Praise for Steven Barthelme

AND HE TELLS THE LITTLE
HORSE THE WHOLE STORY

"Rich in laid-back realism, winsome fantasy, love, art, cats, and surprises. A first-rate first book." **—JOHN BARTH**

"With its unity of situation, *And He Tells the Little Horse the Whole Story* is more than the usual collection, yet not quite a sequence. Small in themselves (the longest is 14 pages), the stories grow in reference and resonance through Mr. Barthelme's considered arrangement. The stories, if not their characters, speak across distances to one another.... exemplars of the minimalist mode..." **—NEW YORK TIMES**

"Steve Barthelme's tone is dead-right; his timing is perfect; and his philosophical stance seems about the best for being here and now. He has put generously from his heart and intellect into every line, so there are moments that linger like good memories. The tales are funny and touching. The telling is always deliberate, always hip, and always entirely his." **—MARY ROBISON**

"Barthelme's wild imagination makes a literary feast ... [A] great creator. And Barthelme is just that. His brothers, Donald and Frederick, already have carved themselves niches in American fiction.... Steve Barthelme appears destined to do the same." **—CHICAGO TRIBUNE**

"To Steve Barthelme's credit, his stories do not remind me of any other Barthelme's. They do, however, accomplish one of the things that short stories have always done best: They trace the subcutaneous, prelingual capillaries of the self's relationship with others and with itself."
—GERALD LOCKLIN, *STUDIES IN SHORT FICTION*

Praise for THE EARLY POSTHUMOUS WORK

"Reading *The Early Posthumous Work* of Steve Barthelme is like having a scintillating conversation with a much smarter friend, a friend with an enterprising sense of wonder and a faithfulness to the ambiguity of life. There's not a moment of self-absorption in these wise, wry, and wildly entertaining essays." **—JOHN DUFRESNE, AUTHOR OF *REQUIEM, MASS.***

"There's a much-vaunted notion of writing as craft, but precisely what is meant by this is not often clear. Steven Barthelme's essays serve as the best of definitions. They afford us the complete pleasure of hearing a thing said with utmost economy and utmost elegance, the two being one. In essay after essay, Barthelme finds memory's perfect pitch.... Crafted by a master." **—ANGELA BALL**

Praise for DOUBLE DOWN
by Frederick Barthelme and Steven Barthelme

"The whole book... is a wonderfully seductive performance—witty, self-aware, at once full of subtle feeling and implacably knowing—a triumph of style over temporary insanity...The Barthelme brothers turned losing into an art." **—A. ALVAREZ, *THE NEW YORK REVIEW OF BOOKS***

"Dazzlingly canny and achingly abject." **—PUBLISHERS WEEKLY**

"A winning book about losing." **—CHRISTOPHER LEHMANN-HAUPT, *THE NEW YORK TIMES***

"May be worth every penny the Barthelmes lost." **—CHICAGO TRIBUNE**

"Talks perceptively and sometimes brilliantly of life, death, family, hope and despair, and money as an expression of these things." **—FAY WELDON, *NEW YORK OBSERVER***

Hush Hush

Hush Hush

STORIES BY

Steven Barthelme

MELVILLE HOUSE
BROOKLYN · LONDON

Hush Hush

First Melville House printing: September 2012

Melville House Publishing
145 Plymouth Street
Brooklyn, NY 11201

www.mhpbooks.com

ISBN: 978-1-61219-159-1

Printed in the United States of America
1 2 3 4 5 6 7 8 9 10

Library of Congress Cataloging-in-Publication Data

Barthelme, Steve.
  Hush hush : stories / Steven Barthelme.
    p. cm.
  ISBN 978-1-61219-159-1
  I. Title.
  PS3552.A7635H87 2012
  813'.54--dc23

                              2012027978

For Melanie

Contents

Siberia

Every eager enquiry elicits exculpatory equivocation, I said, eventually. You tell me, you're the doctor. How would I know. I'm just a child. She was sitting up in the big brown chair trying to get me to tell her what ememtottot means. It's totem-totem, she said, right? What? I said. And then I said, Eureka, that's it, and I pretended to grin. Children grin. You bounce your head up and down and smile like a moron. You're a very mature child, Elliott, she said. Memetottot, I said.

I am not a little adult. I am ten. I am a child and I expect to be treated as a child and it's unkind to treat me as if I'm some kind of curio or freak just because they are bored or something. I know what ememtottot means and no one else does. It's my word, so what? I expect to be bought ice cream cones and talked to stupid and let alone. I can be interested in Siberia or words that begin with "E" without a lot of attention and consultations.

I don't expect to be put in a cage with a fat lady psychologist. But Nietzsche said, E'er twixt expecting und event ist ecstasy. Nietzsche didn't say that. I just made it up. Every time I say Nietzsche said something, the lady psychologist looks at me, trying to figure out whether I made it up. Many words begin with *E*. Eviscerate, Echt, Eldritch, Effervesce, Excreta. Ememtottot. No one but me knows that, what ememtottot means. The lady psychologist does not know.

Nietzsche is some freak dead guy. I won the spelling bee.

First I spelled egregious, and excisable, excalibur, and then mnemonic. I read about Nietzsche in the *World Book*. I play chess. I have an interest in pythons. I am tired of being a special child. I want to chase cars. No, that's wrong, that's dogs.

I don't want to go to a school for the "gifted." Special, gifted, advanced, it all sounds like "freak" to me. They are sending me to this freak school and I'm not adjusting well. I burned myself with a cigarette. Their excuse for locking me in a cage in the basement with a psychologist five days a week. Exculpate Elliott at eventide, excellency. If it's not a cage, why are there bars on the windows?

I was first in class excellence, at my old school. You get a card and that's what it says, First in Class Excellence. In this new school there are much freakier freaks than me; there's an orange kid who looks like Henry Kissinger and a girl who looks like Christiane Amanpour who looks like Mick Jagger. Henry is some professor's kid. Most of the kids in this school are professors' kids or schoolteachers' kids. It makes you wonder. We are all kids whose parents taught them to say "melancholy," and then when they say it, the parents gush and swoon. Give them a dog biscuit. Christiane and I are going to run away together and have sex as soon as we feel like it. Erumpent erotogenesis.

I don't think that reading the dictionary is so strange for a ten year old child, and I am a child. Lots of us do it. There are two kinds of freaks. Freaks who pretend to be normal and freaks who pretend to be freaks. I pretend to be a normal child, but I'm not very good at it. Christiane pretends to be a freak and she is very good at it. You should see her singing "Satisfaction." It is not the freakishness that makes us blue; it's the pretending. You've got to think about it. You're all the time planning, never being. That's why Christiane and I are going

2

to run away. We are going to Siberia. Siberia has been misrepresented, so no one knows about it.

Siberia is a kind of farm with fields and rivers and trees which grow televisions and vines which grow chili cheeseburgers. There's no brown bread in Siberia and no tofu and no yogurt. In Siberia there are no children and no adults, and no one is special or gifted or freak. Everyone has their own personal television set and no one can look at anyone else without their permission. But everyone likes everyone else so they always have permission. Dogs and cats in Siberia can talk and make jokes like everyone else. Squirrels, too. There are no fleas there, and no one gets sick and no one gets shot. In Siberia if someone wants something, they find it, just lying around on the ground. It rains a lot in Siberia, I love rain.

Of course none of this is true. The lady psychologist has been to Russia and so she knows and she has told me that Siberia is a vast icy wasteland. That's what she said, "vast icy wasteland." I said, You sound like the *World Book*. I said, Maybe you're wrong.

In Siberia anyone who wants to be invisible can learn how easy as pie. Words have special powers in Siberia that they don't have in Massachusetts or anywhere in the United States.

I said, Did you see that movie, *One Flew Over the Cuckoo's Nest*? She said, Yep. I swear that's what she said. That made me like her a lot better. I said the psychologists were the bad guys in that movie. She said, Are you going to tell me what ememtottot means? She pronounced it wrong, of course. Totem totem? I said. Why don't I believe you? she said. Because I'm lying? I said. Evidence etches Elliott's eyes.

Anyone who hits a dog or a cat in Siberia is sent home permanently, and Siberian dogs and cats always tell. The principal rivers in Siberia are called the Robert DeNiro and the

Michelle Pfeiffer. The two rivers cross at the exact center of Siberia which is where you go in Siberia if you want to fall in love. Of course everybody wants to fall in love so they go there about once a week.

Sometimes Christiane sings "Get Off of My Cloud."

The lady psychologist said, Do you think psychologists are bad guys, Elliott? I said, Oh no, you're here to help me, and she looked at me like I'd just said something about Nietzsche. No, I mean it, I said. Have you ever actually been to *Siberia*, I said; or was it just Russia? I really *am* here to help you, she said. I thought as much, I said.

I love my mother and father even though this school was their stupid idea. Christiane and I will go to the confluence of the Robert DeNiro and the Michelle Pfeiffer every day, when we get to Siberia. We'll fall in love and kiss and sit on the banks and feed the pythons. Siberian pythons leave the dogs and cats and squirrels be; they eat chili cheeseburgers right off the vines, or ice cream. At higher elevations year round Siberian mountains are crowned in ice cream, which falls in place of snow. Anyone who wants to wear a Band-Aid in Siberia can, but no cut is necessary.

The lady psychologist is all right and she is trying to help me; she's just no good at it. She just can't help me. She said, Why do you think psychologists are bad guys? I laughed, I couldn't help it.

It was just a movie, I said. You're doing your best, I said. I mean, you're helping me, I said. Really, you really are. Don't a lot of kids burn themselves and stuff? Do you really think I need help? Maybe I just hate being in this weird school. Maybe when the headmistress tells us how we're special children and she means we're better, it sounds like worse to me. Maybe I won't ever get to be normal, be normal, now that you have started me out this way. I don't want a headmistress; I want a principal. There isn't any Siberia is there? There is no place to go. If I go to Siberia, Christiane won't be allowed to go with me, will she?

In Siberia the principal mountains are the Diet Coke and Diet Dr. Pepper ranges. In Siberia all people are striped, so there is only one race. In Siberia some people are naturally tall but other people get to be tall one day a week so it doesn't matter. You can't tell them apart. People say, I'm taking a tall day today. People say, Let's dance, and beautiful music starts playing from the sky. People say, I don't want to go to bed yet, and they don't have to. People say, I'm so sleepy, and lie down wherever they are and fall asleep. People say, I love you Elliott, you're not weird at all. People say, Oh, don't go Elliott, not yet. Stay here with us. People say, Ememtottot, and they disappear.

Coachwhip

They were both dead drunk. It had all started inside, the guy had been riding him, talking trash, and then Mitchell began to remember, it was like a procession, people he didn't much like, people who had given him a hard time, guy named Jeff at school, that must've been grammar school, and Robin, and that guy at that sad little dinner party in Boston, who hated Southerners and out of nowhere said, "Yeah, Texas is hell," and wanted to "go outside," the morons always want to "go outside," so this time he had gone, and some women, too, the big one who said, "He can talk," and others, and that's how he'd gotten out here in this oily Fort Worth parking lot behind the bar, the blacktop broken but glistening in the city lights from beyond this ditch or whatever it was, the night wind blowing grit into his eyes, and his nose bloody, kneeling on this guy in the plaid cowboy shirt, watching the loudmouth's eyes roll back, and his hands tight on the guy's neck, he was hardly resisting at all anymore. I'm really no good at this, Mitchell thought—a lucky punch had put the guy down—he sort of stepped into it, shit, this is easy, no wonder they like it so much, I'm going to kill this fucker.

But Mitchell wasn't paying attention. He felt like puking, and his eyes were closing, and his mind was wandering, to a day he had spent with his father—Quinn, his real father—twelve years earlier. He hated his father. Even when his father died, he had not stopped hating him, but only thought, She

7

didn't need fancy doctors to tell her that, when they discovered that his heart had a hole in it. His father had been 45.

• • •

They found the snake in August in a pile of stones in the only shade near a dry creek bed, long and white, lying oddly still, almost stunned, in the midst of big white blocks of limestone. Coachwhip, Quinn thought, and although he knew what it was, he told Mitch to get the book from the car. "We'll look it up," he said. "Watch the barbed wire. Bring the pillowcase, too."

It hadn't been hard to catch. Quinn had gotten his foot on it quickly, before it knew it was prey, or slow maybe from the heat. He'd never seen a slow Coachwhip, except ones that had been in cages for years and had no place to go.

Quinn sat on one of the rocks, holding the snake behind its head. It was about two and a half feet, a young one. Light, the color of sand, but Coachwhips varied a lot; some were red. Looking around at the bleached limestone the creek had cut its bed through, it was obvious why this one was almost white.

Mitch came back from the road.

"What've we got?" Quinn said.

"Just a minute," the boy said. He was sitting on the ground with his short legs splayed out to the black cowboy boots Quinn had bought for him. The boots looked ridiculously large, even though the boy was fat. He hadn't wanted boots, but Quinn had insisted. Got to have boots if we're going snake-hunting next summer.

"Look under 'Racers,'" Quinn said. "Or *Masticophis*." Now he was showing off. Jesus, the Latin name, no less.

The boy noticed. His expression changed, some of the joy went out of it. "You're teaching me," he said. His eyes had gone to slits. His too round face didn't look angry; he just looked like someone else's kid.

"Somebody's got to. Teach you, I mean. C'mon, what is it?"

"It's a Racer?"

"No, but you're close," Quinn said. "Did you find the pictures? Find the pictures."

The boy was back to tearing pages as he flipped through the *Field Guide* in his lap. He brushed the sweat from his forehead with his sleeve. They're so forgiving, Quinn thought. He's already forgiven me.

"Here it is!" Mitch said. "Lemme see it."

Quinn held the snake out to him, and it started to move again, but he tightened his grip.

"Western Coachwhip," the boy said, and then looked down at the color plates in the book again. "Maybe it's Eastern Coachwhip."

"They have maps in the back," Quinn told him. "They show you where each kind lives." When he heard a car, he glanced up, over the rocks and past the mesquite tree by the little creek, toward the road, but it was just a pickup.

When Mitch had checked the ranges of the two varieties and decided—Western—he looked up again. "I can keep him, Daddy?" And then, when he saw his father's hesitation: "You want him?"

Quinn laughed, involuntarily, and shook his head. "No." He shook his head again. "I was just thinking maybe it'd be better to let him go. You know, sometimes they die, you put them in a cage." But he felt uncomfortable, telling the boy he couldn't have what he wanted, and he tried to find some feeling behind the words, but all he thought was, Sometimes they die when a car runs over them, sometimes they die when a hawk catches them, sometimes…

"I can keep him, then?" Mitch said. "I'll take good care of him. He won't die."

"Before winter," Quinn said, "you have to let him go. He won't make it through the winter."

The boy's nod, as he reached for the snake, was so slight that Quinn wasn't sure he'd even seen it.

"Mitchell?"

"Okay," the boy said.

"October first. And here. We'll come out here and let him go. Okay?"

"All right."

With luck, Quinn thought, it'll make it to October. And they walked back to the car.

●　●　●

Son of a bitch used to come by once a week, or once a month, and pretend to be my father. Teach me things. He was a Boy Scout all right.

The guy in the cowboy shirt started to rise, brought a hand around and caught Mitchell's ear so hard he thought he was going to black out, and he slammed the guy's head back down against the blacktop. "Fucker," he said. "You miserable drunken slut." He held the cowboy's head down against the pavement, but the man was still.

If I kill him, Mitchell thought, they'll put me in Huntsville, I'm not rich enough to get out of it. He felt weak, and tired. His ear hurt. I shouldn't drink, he thought, not so much. We took the snake back and put it in that aquarium. It died, later. Never took me to let it go. He was afraid of me.

• • •

Joanne was waiting in the front yard, pretending to be watering, but Quinn knew that she was there because they were late, so he was surprised she didn't complain, about the time or even about the child's new pet. Instead she asked him in.

"Stewart?" Quinn said.

"He's not here," she said, shutting off the hose. She was wearing sandals, and a light cotton dress, busy, blue marked with black.

She had moved in with somebody, but not until five years after the divorce, and by that time they had developed an easy friendship, so that she would say, We had a miserable marriage, but a happy divorce. Stewart did something with computers and telephone systems. In the wide, light living room, Quinn settled opposite her, on the arm of a big off-white armchair. She was sitting on a couch.

"You're sure it's not dangerous?" she said, when Mitch had disappeared into the back of the house with the snake.

Quinn shook his head. "If it bites him, put some peroxide on it. Just like any other scratch."

"Well, maybe he'll learn some responsibility," she said.

Quinn looked at the carpet. "Jesus, I wouldn't want to be a kid again. Always getting taught stuff."

She looked at him.

"I didn't mean anything by it," he said.

Her silence was worse, he thought, than any of the things he was imagining her saying, things about responsibility, about his being still more kid than man, about what he should be doing for his child that Stewart was now doing and how good Stewart was at it.

"I just meant that sometimes I wonder whether what I'm teaching him is right."

"You have the leisure," she said. Then she looked down. "I'm sorry. I wanted to talk to you, I really did. And now we've gotten into this. It was a rotten thing to say. I'm sorry." She shrugged, and showed him her open hands.

"None taken," he said, and took her hand, releasing it quickly. "It's just talk. Relax."

"Tell me something, Quinn," she said, and looked away. "When you were… when you used to sleep with Marianne and come home to me, how did you feel about me? I mean, did you—" She smiled. "I don't know what I mean."

"You mean Stewart is…"

She shook her head, slowly, and her look was tentative, wary. "Me," she said, and looked up.

"You want an answer?" He waited for her to nod, but she didn't, just kept staring, so he looked away. "Well, it's not very useful, but what I felt was—I loved you both." He smiled. "I still love you. Don't know where she is. So it goes, I guess."

"You're right. It's not very useful." The boy said something, from the back, coming down the hall toward the living room. Outside it was beginning to get dark. She looked toward the hall. "Stewart is sweet," she said.

Quinn rolled his eyes at her.

• • •

Mitchell got up. Some kid came out of a door in the back of the dark bar, carrying a silver tub, poured it out, looked at them, walked back inside. The cowboy opened his eyes and got up on his elbows, then his knees, then stood.

Mitchell looked at him, vague, uncertain, and then he stopped caring. The cowboy began swinging, hitting him, first softly, clumsily, and then, when Mitchell just stood with his arms hanging, harder and harder until Mitchell's cheek was cut below his eye and his nose was gushing blood and he wobbled and then fell. The cowboy spit. No wonder they like it so much, Mitchell thought. It's easy. He was afraid I wouldn't like him. Didn't know what he was doing. He didn't have a clue. And then he died. Mitchell smiled, and closed his eyes. That must've come as a shock.

Heaven

The poet delicately picks his nose while talking on my telephone, his old abraded sneakers up on my coffee table. This is authentic behavior, the poet is proving that he is a poet, at least I assume that's what he's doing. He glances up at me and then continues his picking and his conversation. "*In this country!*" he shouts into the receiver. It's a joke; he is talking to a poet about a poet. Much laughter. He puts something in the ashtray.

Is he a good poet? He is thought by poetry authorities to be a good poet, but what do they know? I love him, but this does not blind me to his poetry. In the poem he wrote about me after my death, I wrote the only good line. He was quoting me, but the attribution was somewhat vague. I was dead twenty-one minutes before he got to the typewriter.

My sister, inexplicably, doesn't want to sleep with the poet, though I have offered him to her on several occasions. My sister said she'd design her own therapy, thank you. He looks like he needs a bath, she said, he looks a touch gamey, gamey is the word. Poets prize that look, I said. He sleeps with women by the dozens, I said. Golly, she said. Poets get them down any way they can—liquor, B-pluses, enigmas. This isn't winning, she said. Making up for high school, I said.

Heaven. In heaven, no hardwood floors and no baseball and poets caught talking about sports get the rack. Yesterday I saw Jesus in a leather hat.

Here is what the poet is saying on the telephone: "Back

together? Really? In Vermont she and Bruno and Tige got na-
ked in the lake and *alors, voila...*" Another part of it is like this:
"*...and so her pants were on inside out, har har har...*" It's a long
distance call.

Here is what the poet says in the classroom: "Be inexpli-
cable, but not inexplicatable. Be emendatious but not cemen-
tatious (Not in my dictionary; suspect that's a coinage). Be
abominable yet abdominal. Make it newt. (I hear poorly, so
this could have been 'Make it new,' although he loathes Pound;
it may have been 'Make a note'—sometimes he feigns a boffo
French accent.) Oh, and see me after class, Caitlin, Feta, An Li,
Eschscholzia, Daisy, Zinnia, Dahlia."

Before being admitted into heaven I suffered ninety days
in purgatory, which is how I know he wrote a poem about
me after I died. It was okay. Some people get the exercise bike.
Apparently there's no hell.

The poet drives a Land Rover, of course. Loves his wife.
Rubs dogs with great gusto.

In heaven Scotch is blessedly harmless, and my back has
finally stopped hurting, and my body's really buffed. Didn't
require crunches, either, which are what I got into poetry to
avoid. But the poet has written, "All a poet really needs is a
six-pack and a six-pack. Grolsch—and really ripped abs," he
explained. "But Grolsch is expensive!" I cried. "In *this* country," he said.

Heaven resembles a very large Days Inn where God is
always wandering around saying, "Have you seen Jesus? Have
you seen Jesus?" They argue constantly. Jesus says, "'I will de-
stroy the wisdom of the wise?'" alluding to something his Father said (1st Corinthians, I looked it up) and snaps his fingers.
"Fundamentally unserious, Dad."

"I guess I should *frown* more," his Father says, and gives

a weary look. The building, heaven, goes on as far as the eye can see, into the clouds. In the lobby in the morning an enormously long white tablecloth appears, with coffee and one lemon Danish, which renews itself endlessly. Angels are everywhere, dancing.

The poet's life has been lived on the edge, in several countries, in his friends' apartments. The poet spent twelve years working for the John Deere Corporation, two weeks in law school in Boston, a night and day in jail on a vagrancy charge (inspiration for the poems, later, in *I Fought the Law*), and once played tambo in a rock band. The band got him started in poetry when he discovered deep feeling and first wore a perm. "Candy from a bebe," he says of that period.

"Only women understand me," he says. With the help of a wealthy coal widow he started *The New Bituminous Review* and filled it with uncanny and haunting work by the editors of other magazines. Then for three years he fearlessly walked up and down Sixth Avenue, filling out grant applications, winning nine. "It's a poet eat poet world out there," he says.

They don't only argue. Last week, God and Jesus were in the main lobby, rolling on the carpet, laughing about Hell. "Who could have known that they'd take that *seriously?*" God said. "They've been worrying about that for two *thousand* years!" he snorted, and fell into convulsions of laughter. "And—and—" Jesus said, wiping tears from his shining eyes, "and we were only *kidding*! God, they must think we're mean!" And they walked off slapping their foreheads and kneecaps and Jesus' hat fell off. His eyes are intensely beautiful, blue. Very tall.

The poet is thought to have a very good gamey look, I told my sister. One of the top five, among contemporary American poets. His wife won't mind, I said, because he's an artist. What is his poetry about? she said. Anguish, I said. Black woe. Raw unashamed passion. Black Lung. A number of his newest poems shockingly unmask the pylorus, where a valve inextricably links man's stomach to his small intestine.

My death came about in this way: I poisoned myself, with loathing. And envy, there was some envy. Mostly loathing.

The poet is off the phone. He has a legal pad and a blue and black German pencil, working probably on "Reflux." It's a new one in the Los Angeles Lakers series. "Overweight and eager..." the poem begins. He pauses, pencil to his lips. He is thinking. I ask if he will stay to dinner, and he slams the pencil down, enraged. "Oh, Christ," he says, "can't you see I'm working? What're you having? I'll invite Peesha, Pasha, and Tony. It's all ruined now," he says. The pencil is very beautiful. He picks up the telephone.

Jesus comes over to me when I'm out on a chaise beside one of the pools; he's holding a fat red book in one hand and in the other, two lemonade cans from the vending machine. He hands me one. Frigid. All around us, people are getting to their feet. Music is playing somewhere.

"A hat?" I say. "You're never in a hat in the pictures."

"I'm two thousand years old," Jesus says, and pats the leather hat. "I'll wear a hat if I feel like it." He gives a droll smile. "I have you down here for loathing and envy," he says, looking up from the red ledger. "You must forgive him."

"There's nothing to forgive," I say, and take a drink. It's Handel, the music.

"Bo, I'm Jesus. Why are you bothering to lie to me?"

"Yes, sorry, I forgot. Gosh, this lemonade is cold."

Jesus sighs. "That's a nice touch, that 'Gosh.' A little foolish, considering that you're already in heaven. Still, 'God hath chosen the foolish things of the world to confound the wise.'" He shrugs. "It's in 1st Corinthians."

"That'd be Chapter 1," I say, "verse 27?"

He glances sharply at me for a second but recovers, nods, and slaps the red book on his pants. "You must forgive him."

"Okay. I forgive him."

Jesus looks at me with his brilliant eyes. It's the sort of long, theatrically patient look one gets not from a father but from a beloved older brother.

"Okay, I don't forgive him. Okay." The breeze in heaven is soft, sweet, smells delicately of oranges.

The poet wants to write good poetry, I know he does. He does not think of himself as a dull, careerist predator and sham. He could be a counterfeit and write great poetry at the same time, perhaps. He wants to know awe. He wants to have important things to say to his fellows, to make cold souls warm, to ease hurt, to praise love, to give hope to the despairing and companion to the lonely, to hold the breath of wisdom in his hand for an instant, to add to what we have. He wants to *see*. Even a blind squirrel finds a . . . No, nevermind that.

"Jesus, this is hard. This is hard," I say, "Jesus."

His eyes are terrible.

Interview

Three weeks after Terry Quinn quit his fancy job at the law firm, got in his car, left Atlanta and drove a thousand miles back to Texas, he went to a party. He had been living at a motel since he'd arrived in Austin, and for three weeks had spoken to no one but gas station clerks, waitresses, and supermarket checkers. The law office was looking better and better, in hindsight. Maybe, he thought, running away from home at thirty-two wasn't such a great idea.

He'd been told about the party by a woman named Liz, an attractive half-Japanese woman who he had met once ten years earlier. It happened that she worked at the branch library where he had spent a long afternoon reading some hopeless career-change book with an embarrassingly silly name. The ten minutes talking to her was so pleasant to him that even though he usually hated and feared parties, he had decided to go. He had considered offering to take her, but decided against it, unsure of what her casual "You should come" might have meant. So he went back to the motel and thought about her and waited for nine o'clock.

The party was in a big stone house beside a lake, and music and people spilled out onto the courtyard and a paved area adjacent to it. Liz was only there for half an hour or so, but she was even more enchanting in the evening than she had been in the afternoon. They stood together outside in the night air, talking about law school, which she had quit, and cats, or kittens, which she was giving away. As she spoke, she absently buttoned and unbuttoned the cuff of her sleeve. After talking for a while Quinn managed to make a date to take her to dinner the following Tuesday, which as it turned out was her birthday. When she had gone he lingered, watching people drink and dance, remembering why he didn't like parties, sometimes entering into brief conversations with friendly drunks.

One was a man named Allen Powell, a chunky, hard-faced guy who drew from people an urgent and automatic deference and who seemed to own a number of businesses—an apartment complex, at least two restaurants, a delivery service, and others, some less savory, apparently. Powell had a dull, distracted, almost pensive expression as he stood outside with Quinn, staring out at the dark lake, watching lights ripple on the water.

"So, what do you do?" he asked, and when Quinn said that he was out of work, Powell offered him a job in a car repair shop—completely indifferent to his meager experience—and instructed him to talk to a man named Rollo, or failing that, a drunk named Lancaster. Quinn laughed, thanked him, and left. As he was walking off, he thought he heard someone say, "Well, fuck you," and as he turned back to look, his shoe slipped on a stone step and he twisted his knee. Powell had disappeared.

Quinn had just rented a small apartment, but hadn't yet quit the motel, and the twenty-one hundred dollars cash money he had brought with him from Atlanta was almost gone. The initial exhilaration of ditching his whole life had shortly worn thin, and his few attempts to find work had been as fruitless as they had been desultory, consisting mostly of studying the want ads and remembering that he didn't know how to do anything but tax law, and that even if he wasn't good at it, no one had ever seemed to notice. It bewildered him. He was a fraud, but no one cared.

He had resolved not to do law anymore because this feeling of fraudulence about work, which everyone seemed to feel but most people forgot or shrugged off, bothered him unduly. The fraud had extended past work, though, to his purchase on everything in his life, including the wife from whom he was separated, and whose diagnosis was that he had unrealistic expectations. She had once suggested what she called "What Did You Expect Therapy."

Three weeks in Austin, where he had gone to school, had reminded Quinn how much he had depended on his job, fraud or no. The city had not changed much, but it wasn't his anymore.

During the day, driving his old car, he felt the shiny new Acuras and Saabs and minivans pushing him off their clean streets and freeways. He would signal and then switch lanes, thinking, They belong here. Sometimes at night he stood at the front window of the motel room, holding the curtain aside, watching headlights of the cars on the streets, envying the drivers their jobs, houses, children, garden hoses, and the newspaper which appeared on their driveways each morning.

So even though Powell was clearly some kind of drug baron or celebrity felon, a few days after the party Quinn decided to become a mechanic. He had fixed some cars, once. Even got paid a couple of times. Anyway, he was running out of money.

But he felt things were looking up. The utilities were on now in his tiny new apartment and he had got the telephone turned on. And the woman from the library held out the hope that women always did, that everything might be different.

It was Tuesday, not much past noon, when he limped up

23

to the motel office to settle the bill, thinking, Move out, move in, get a job, go to dinner, fall in love, Wednesday.

The day clerk, a Spanish man, balding, very tall, was sitting on a stool, watching a Mexican television show and reading a newspaper. He rose as Quinn walked into the lobby, and standing, he looked like NBA material.

"Through tomorrow noon," Quinn said. "What does it come to?"

The clerk pulled out the bill, unfolded it on the counter, bent over and wrote furiously with a gold pen. He twirled the bill around.

Quinn looked at the six hundred dollars left in his wallet, took out a credit card. He assumed that by now his wife had already cancelled all the cards—I would, he thought—but it was worth a shot. "Try this."

The man nodded. "You got a weekly rate," he said, and laughed.

Quinn looked at him.

He smiled. "We don't use it very often. But we got it so you got it." He flashed the credit card through the slot, and then ran off the slip and handed the card back. After a moment, he shook his head in a showy sort of way, and said, "I am sorry, but could I try this card again? The machine, it's—"

"That's all right," Quinn said. "I'll pay cash."

The clerk tore the credit card slip in half and handed it across the counter, took the five hundred dollar bills. "You stay here a long time. We hope you enjoy your stay," he said, and wrote _Paid_ at the base of the bill.

"I like motels," Quinn said.

The guy turned back around, smiling. "You know, I do too. I take a room here, too. Sometimes I stay a week, two weeks." He nodded, settled back on his stool. "This a great

24

job. Nobody believes me, you know, but this a great job." He smiled and rubbed both hands over the hair left at the sides of his head. "I am sorry about the Visa card."

Quinn laughed. "My mistake," he said, and waved the card. "It's..." He blinked and looked at it. "Broken," he said, finally, and shrugged. On his way out, he bought a paper. The knee he had twisted on the steps at the party felt better, almost well, as he walked the narrow sidewalk in front of the rooms.

Back in his room, he remembered reading the want ads, or trying to, the jobs he couldn't do or had never heard of, "Junior Liaison Engineer, nut test, P-test specializations," other weird notices written in code. Nurses. References, he thought. Must have own tools. He shuddered. I used to have potential. But you probably can't have "potential" at thirty-two.

This a great job, he thought. Jesus, what must that be like? The Lord is my shepherd, I shall not work. No, not it. He slipped his car keys off the night table. Happily, he thought, there's a path of least resistance available. I used to like fooling with cars, anyway.

The Car Clinic was out in a field under a too blue sky in a depressed part of town near the intersection of three high-ways. The road in front of it ran between alternating fields of tawny weeds and low industrial brick buildings inside hurri-cane fences. The full name was Lancaster Car Clinic and Fine Auto Detailing, Inc. It occupied three steel buildings each with a concrete apron spreading out in front, and between the concrete slabs were two alleys of red mud, dry and hard now, flecked with scrub grass. An old Checker taxicab was parked at the back of one of these mud alleys, along with two weathered

VW's, and some seats, fenders, batteries, starters, and lumps covered with thin black plastic which looked big enough to be engines or transmissions. The farthest of the three tin buildings had the big doors shut. Four kids, three skinny boys and a very tall girl, were sitting around just inside the nearest steel shed, passing a joint and laughing. One blond boy with rock 'n' roll hair was holding a big silver wrench in his hand.

"Help you?" he said, when Quinn walked up. He looked about eighteen.

"Help you?" the girl said, mimicking him. Striking blue eyes, made more striking by her hair—boy cut, dyed black. She was wearing black leggings with big holes in them, under a T-shirt, even though it was nearly 95 degrees.

"Shut up, Dix. Don't mind her."

The girl was staring. "I *love* your shoes," she said. "Are they Bally? What size are they? They might fit me."

"Bigfoot," one of the others said.

"I'm looking for a guy named Rollo," Quinn said, leaning down, rubbing his knee with the heel of his hand. "Allen sent me."

"*Wooooo*," the kids said, in unison.

"*Al-len* sent him," the girl said. "What'd you, just get back from Huntsville?"

"Shut up, Dix," the blond kid said again.

"He's not very pretty," she said. "Most of the guys from Huntsville are rhinopretty." She grabbed at the remains of the joint, which the first kid held up out of her reach. "C'mon, gimme," she said. She frowned. "You are acting like a child."

"My name is Morton," the blond kid said. "Mort." He handed the girl the joint, pointed with his wrench. "Dix. And Dave, and Patricio. Rollo's never here, really. Just as well. He couldn't fix a car if his life depended on it."

"*Woooo*," the others said again.

"Like, quality control," the one called Dave said.

"You couldn't either, Mort," Patricio said. He looked at Quinn. "Don't think he knows how to use that wrench. Yesterday, he asked me what a head gasket was."

"I knew," Mort said.

"What about… Lancaster?" Quinn said. "Someone named Lancaster around?" It dawned on him that that was the name on the place.

"Get Bubbles," Dave said.

"Davy," Mort said. "I told you not to talk like that."

"It's ugly, Davy," the black-haired girl said, with a studied look away. "Why be ugly?"

Mort looked suddenly tired, as if he could barely raise his arm to point to the next steel shed. "Next door," he said. "Stay away from the detailing shop—the last building? They don't like it when you hang around there."

"Thanks," Quinn said, and started across the hardened mud alley toward the second steel building. Even these children belong here, he thought, wondering at their quirky serenity, recalling his own childhood, its unease. He wondered how old he must look to them, and then he thought about Liz the librarian, wondered how old she thought he was.

Inside the second shed there were two Hondas, an old Oldsmobile, and a new blue Pontiac in the bays. Lancaster was underneath the Pontiac, a big man in worn shoes and stiff blue coveralls. "With you in a minute," he said. He sounded black. Quinn looked around.

The place was uncommonly tidy, even clean. A tall red tool chest, on wheels, stood beside the Pontiac, and a fat black wire ran to the trouble light the guy had under it. The Olds was up on a lift, hovering a foot off the ground. Beside one

Honda, pieces of something were laid out between two red rags like an exploded diagram. A long counter ran three feet high along the corrugated steel rear wall, and above it and above three or four old Pirelli calendars, a string of windows, the glass, amazingly, clear, sparkling.

"So what can I do you?" the black guy said, standing, wiping his hands on another red rag. He looked past Quinn for a car. "What sort of problem you got?" He was easily six four. His eyes were streaked and red and sagged a little and his arms, his belly, even his cheeks looked heavy and soft, not so much fat, Quinn thought, as uncared for.

"I'm looking for work," Quinn said. "That so," the guy said. "That so." He was looking at Quinn's shoes. "Well, you need to talk to Rollo, or a man named Powell."

"My name's Quinn." He held out his hand.

Lancaster shook hands. "Well, Mr. Quinn, we're pretty well fixed right now. I got four kids working next door." He pointed.

"Actually, Allen Powell sent me over," Quinn said. "He said I should talk to you, if Rollo wasn't around. You're Mr. Lancaster, aren't you?"

The black guy laughed. "I'm Bub. I used to be Mr. Lancaster at one time, sure was. Then I got sent to Viet Nam, and then I got sent to Raiford, that's in Florida. Since then, I'm Bub." He looked at Quinn, appraising him. "You know about cars?"

"Not a whole lot. Been working in a shop for a year in Atlanta."

Lancaster laughed. "That so, you've been wearing some fine leather gloves." He laughed again, saw Quinn looking up at him. "Show me your hands," he said. He motioned for them. "Go on, let me see your hands."

Quinn held his hands out. Lancaster took them, turned them palms up, stared at them, looked up at Quinn, smiling, and let them fall.

"Yeah, okay," Quinn said. "Yeah. Maybe it was fifteen years ago. It was a while back. All this electronic stuff, I don't know anything about it." He looked back toward the first building. "But, you know, I met your help. The boys and girls?"

Lancaster shook, laughing, tried to stop, couldn't. "Yeah, Rollo hires them. They're sort of... trainees," he said. "Tire needs changing, dope needs smoking, we bring them in." He laughed again. "Actually 'Tricio is a fair hand and so's Davy. Other two are strictly Blue Lagoon."

Two Porsches, lipstick red, roared up the street and turned in at the third building and stopped. A small, dowdy young woman, in glasses and an old, empire-waisted dress, stepped out of the near car and trudged inside as a garage door went up.

Lancaster turned back to him. "Let's see, Mr. Quinn. I wonder if you know anything about fixing cars. Can you do us a brake job, say? On this Olds here?" He petted the rear fender of the big yellow car. "Certainly would save me some trouble. Little hundred dollar job."

"Right now?"

Lancaster looked at him. "You want a job?" He started to rub at the corner of his eye with a finger, then stopped to rub the finger clean on his blue suit. "It's already up, and there's an impact wrench on the floor there and all the tools you'll need in the tower." He pointed to the fancy red toolbox. "Bottom two drawers."

"What's the matter with it?"

"It doesn't stop."

Quinn looked at him, trying to remember brakes.

"Okay, you tell me," Lancaster said. "Man says the brakes are bad. Car'll stop but it takes a good long time. Fluid's low but still okay."

"Warning lights?" Quinn said. He crouched down next to the front wheel, wincing, and looked across under the car at the inside of the other front tire, then in around at the near one, checked the back tires. "It's not leaking at the wheels. Master cylinder leaking?"

The big man, watching, smiled, shook his head.

"Just the front pads, then," Quinn said. He stood up again. "Right?"

The guy laughed, nodded. "That's right. Just do the front. I'll put the shoes on the back later. There're no leaks. The master's almost new."

"Why are you going to do the back, if it's just the front?"

Lancaster looked at him, trying to simplify what he had to say enough to make it comprehensible to a soft-handed, but maybe not hopeless apprentice. "Look here, Shadetree, if the front's worn a lot the back's worn a little, you know? They got a metering valve on here, supposed to even up the braking—it only half works. Any time car's been driven, the wear's uneven. So we start them over even, it's a equilibrium thing." He held out his two pale rough palms, as if weighing something. "And I don't want the man back a week on with a car I fixed that don't stop. This used to be my shop. But that ain't it..." He sighed, shook his big head, and looked out toward the road in front of the place. "Bad work makes me feel bad. You know what I mean?"

Quinn looked at the big yellow Oldsmobile floating in the oily air of the place. How hard can it be, he thought. Just brakes. He remembered doing brakes in parking lots on cars up on scissor jacks and bleeding them into Coke bottles. He remembered sitting around in clubs with people from the law office where the bar tab ran to three hundred dollars.

"What's the matter?" the black man said.

"I'm used to doing this on Volkswagens."

"'bout the same thing," Lancaster said. "Only these just have one piston. And you take the caliper off to do the work. Two bolts." He held up two thick fingers.

Quinn looked past him, at the front wheel. "Doesn't make sense. How can they do it with one piston? How do they equalize the pads, balance the pressure?"

"Caliper floats. Whole thing. Piston's squeezing against itself. Jesus H. You're sure enough shadetree, aren't you?"

"I can fix this." Quinn pointed across to the Pontiac. "You can go on back under there. Out of my way. I'll have this sucker finished in an hour." He walked over to the impact wrench lying on the concrete and picked it up.

"Okay, Shadetree," Lancaster said. "But the book says the job is two units." He started walking back toward the office at the end of the building. "That's *half* hour. You want a coke?"

Quinn pulled the trigger to hear the power wrench's rolling scream. He looked over to the next parking lot, but they had pulled the Porsches inside.

It took him the full hour, getting the feel of the tools, taking care to keep parts clean and free of dirt and grit, double checking that this moved freely or that fit the way it was supposed to. He liked the work, the feel of the tools and the grease smell and the intoxication any physical work brings, if you don't do too much. The machine had a sort of pride in itself, an elegance of operation, and the work a sort of coherence.

Things had reasons for being the way they were. The tools had their own coherence, an invented logic. Someone just made it up, like someone had just made up the law, but if a bolt was the wrong thread, there was no arguing it, and having twice as much money, or twice as much attorney, didn't change the fact. But that wasn't it either.

He liked the law still, really, the arrogance of its made-up-ness, the handsome job men had done with it. It wasn't law that had set him down on this cool concrete with the grime on his fingers and grit in his eye and idiot grin on his face. The law was all right. And the money was all right. And the clock with the big numbers, he thought. I loved that clock.

In fact, he liked all the yuppie stuff. Toaster, fat sweatshirts, microwave, wok. He liked walking into everyone's house and finding that same red electric wok. But the price was pretending to be someone out of *Fortune* crossed with someone out of the *Utne Reader* married to someone from *Vogue* crossed with *Bulletin of the National Anti-vivisection Society*. Pretending to know things. In almost all ways an easy, pleasant life, plus profit-sharing, except for the pretending, the sensation of walking around in an extra skin, like some weird deep sea diver who has forgotten why he came here. But it's not the law, Quinn reminded himself. This is the way I felt in elementary school.

He twisted the torque wrench, set at 37 ft-lbs., until it slipped internally, checked it, then tightened the other mounting bolt on the caliper. The work had taken him too long, but it had gone easily. Only once had he had to ask advice, about a rubber dust boot, and Lancaster himself had had trouble getting it in. Lancaster had left whatever he had been working on for later and done the rear brakes on the old Oldsmobile while Quinn was working on the front. He had finished sometime earlier even though he had rebuilt the wheel cylinders as well as replacing the brake shoes. Now he was sitting on a stool by the long counter at the back, drinking vodka and coughing.

"You done?" he said, when he saw Quinn set the black torque wrench down on the concrete. "Finally?" He raised the broad little pint of vodka, laughing, then pointed at a length of clear plastic hose and a Coke bottle standing on the counter. "Now we got to bleed them. Why don't you get in the car and pump the pedal for me?"

"What?" Quinn said. "Why do I get in the car? Why don't you get in the car?" He looked at the green bottle. "That's very technological equipment you got there."

Lancaster looked at him, stood up from the stool, shook his head. "Okay, Shadetree, I'll get in the car." He took another drink. "Here," he said, and held out the vodka.

Quinn took it, glanced at him, wiped the neck of the vodka on his shirt and took a drink. He wiped his lips with his sleeve and handed the bottle back, pointing with it at the driver's door. Then he fetched the hose and the Coke bottle and sat down by the right front wheel.

The front wheels went quickly, there was no air in the lines, but the rear took some doing. Lancaster had cleaned up the wheel cylinders, including the bleeder bolts, so that they turned like butter, there wasn't any feel in the threads.

That's what Quinn told himself anyway, when on the last wheel, with the bubbles of air just about out of the line and clear brake fluid coming down it every time he opened the bleeder, he snapped it closed too smartly and twisted off the top half.

"Oh, Christ," he said, looking at the torn metal in the jaws of the locking pliers. "Shit." He stared at the other half lodged in the wheel cylinder, and his shoulders sank.

After a minute, Lancaster got out of the car and walked around to Quinn, sitting at the right rear wheel. He looked huge. "There a problem?" He coughed into his fist.

Quinn held up the pliers, showing him the half bleeder bolt.

He laughed. "You're taking this too hard, Shadetree. Try an Easy Out. I'll get one. It's probably too soft, but you might get it that way."

Quinn was still staring at the pieces of the torn bolt. "I always used to do this. Overtighten things. Try too hard. Being a good boy."

"Look, you messed up. Let's not make it Biblical." Lancaster looked at the vodka bottle, shook it. "Shoo," he said. "I think they don't put a whole pint in these things." He shook it again.

It took another twenty minutes to get the broken bolt out and replace it, re-bleed the rear brakes. When Quinn started the hydraulic lift up instead of down and then jerked the lever back in a panic, letting the Oldsmobile drop a foot onto the concrete, Lancaster laughed until he started to cough again. He raised the car back up and slid underneath to check it. "There's a big can of Gojo in the bathroom down there," he said from under the car. "Hand cleaner, you know."

Quinn shuffled off, smiling, toward the bathroom next to the small office, watching his soft charcoal gray slip-on shoes kick out in front of him. I'm home, he thought. I'll move into the apartment, subscribe to the paper. Get a library card. Some regular shoes.

Lancaster was leaning against the other car looking at the yellow Oldsmobile when Quinn walked back up. "Well, I guess you're hired now," Lancaster said, watching Quinn wiping his hands on a rag. "If you want."

"After screwing up twice?" Quinn said. "Bleeder bolt *and* the lift?" He tossed the red rag into a gray steel barrel of rags on the concrete under the back counter and looked toward the Oldsmobile, frowning. There wasn't any obvious damage from its fall. It had bounced.

"Wouldn't mind having an adult around here."

"Probably be more trouble to you than—"

Lancaster sighed. "Look, white boy, you're hired. You been hired since you said the two magical words. Allen Powell. But I'm mighty happy to have this brake work done. You want the job or don't you?"

"Words don't sound magic," Quinn said, standing beside him, looking out at the road.

"They magic around here," Lancaster said.

"What's the story on this other building?" Quinn said, and nodded toward it. "The detailing shop?"

"Ain't no other building," Lancaster said, and looked out, searching. "You see some other building?"

"No, I guess not." Quinn glanced over at the building that wasn't.

"You want the job?"

"Yeah, I guess so."

"What do you really do?" Lancaster said.

"Guess I fix cars."

"You guess an awful lot, Shadetree."

"That's for sure," Quinn said.

The other man laughed, a quiet shaking laugh in his round cheeks and thick arms. He crossed his arms in front of him and sighed. "I'm going out this evening, do some drinking? Maybe shoot some pool? You'd be welcome to come."

"Later," Quinn said. "Yeah, I want to later. Tonight I got to see a lady. It's her birthday."

"You're younger than I thought," Lancaster said. "But that's okay."

"So did I crack something? Is the Olds okay?"

Lancaster shrugged. "Looks all right to me."

"Good." Quinn laughed. "Hate to have to tell him, Yeah, well, we did the brakes on this pile—but then we cracked both axles."

"Wouldn't have to tell him. He'd already know," Lancaster said, looking out at the yellow weeds standing high in the fields on the other side of the road. "That's my car there." He shook his head, and a smile curled at the corner of his eye. "My car." He nodded and glanced over toward the back wall. Summer sunlight cut in through the pristine windows above the counter. Five o'clock.

Quinn slipped his shoes off and reached down to get them.

Lancaster frowned. "What are you doing, brother? Making yourself to home?"

"I figure Dix'd like these shoes." Quinn said, straightening up again, shoes hanging from his fingers. He stopped, looked up. "Stuff some newspaper in there."

"Gal is a fashion plate, ain't she?" Lancaster said, and nodded his big head, agreeing with himself. "Uh huh."

The New South:
Writing the *Newsweek* Short Story

The place was full of hicks. They were eating tires, all-terrain, it's a local delicacy. It tastes like fried chicken. They were short, the ones that weren't larger than life. Okay, well, so the guy didn't say, "Knee-caps to a gee-raffe," exactly. He said, "short," that the old guy was short, but that wouldn't have been very *colorful* and everybody knows there are a lot of colorful folks down South. So when I wrote the piece, I kinda said he said something he didn't say, exactly. But gee-raffe is what he meant. Somebody did say that once, it's not like I made it up; I had an English teacher once who said that, Southern guy. There is no such thing as objectivity, I mean we all agree on that, right? He looked like a guy who was thinking, *Knee-caps*.

The stuff about the steroid poodle and the pit bull? No, that's just the way it happened. Pit bull didn't know what hit him. Little furry fella. Damnedest thing I ever saw. And that short old guy just smiled and spit tobacco juice into his Dixie cup and collected his money, got his poodle, and drove away in that Cadillac. There wasn't anyone there named "Velvet Skinned Annie" though—I stole that from an Elmore Leonard book I was reading. Damn good book, a Western. They made a movie out of it, with Paul Newman, good movie. Poodle had some abs, I tell you.

Well, and it was a pretty big poodle, like the size of a

python. Well, it could've been a python. I couldn't see too well, I was in the bar, watching on closed-circuit TV, and on the screen all you could see were all those good ole boys in plaid shirts crowded around, hollering and waving bills in the air. This was right after the Rattlesnake Roundup. Tastes just like fried chicken.

Come to think of it, there was no poodle in the Cadillac, when the old guy left. He was sort of a young old guy. Left town with Velvet Skinned Annie hanging all over him and the "deppity sherff" right on his tail. Come to think of it, it was a Lexus, or a Cherokee, one of those. I've never actually been to that bar, but my brother told me about it. I'd've had to leave the apartment to go to that bar. Wait a minute, I think the magazine's calling.

It wasn't really a deputy sheriff, it was an ATF agent. Actually… nevermind. Maybe the python was in the trunk. This is where the story gets a little hazy; I had to fill in some blanks. I did interview the PR guy from the state gaming commission and he does have a slot machine on his desk, one of those like you can buy at Circuit City. My brother told me.

I interviewed the guy by telephone. He did say the thing about giving a "rat's ass," that's verbatim—"Son, I don't give a redneck rat's ass whether some snake tore the peewaddle out of some moongoose." He didn't say "Son," I polished a little. I hadn't told him it was a mongoose, I had said "mongrel," but nobody pays attention nowadays. "Peewaddle" is a word my daughter got at that Catholic school, isn't it great?

If I had a brother, I'd name him Mozart. Mozart P. Concerto, that's my real last name, Concerto. We're Italian. It wasn't a mongoose—or a "moongoose!" God damn these people are colorful—it was more of a mouse-type creature. The magazine sent me to check on the pandas, how they were doing, one of them's been sick, it was some kind of Red Chinese thing, and while I was waiting for the curator I wandered into the reptile house, and a bunch of the staff—they were Pakistanis mostly, sounded like the BBC in there—were hanging around while they fed some of the snakes.

They *were* wearing plaid shirts, though. Except one had on this gorgeous topcoat. It was a big mother, bull snake or something. I was on deadline, and under a wee bit of pressure; the goddamn magazine hadn't used anything of mine in eleven years. I started thinking, What if I maybe just *ooonch* this a little. I have never, ever, done anything like this before, understand. Maybe this little ole mouse is a dog, some kind of colorful, Southern dog…You're under a certain pressure to come up with startling or fresh ideas, you know, a vision thing. May sound simple, but it isn't. Trick is to make sure they look exactly like the old ideas.

Anyway, the Pakistani, the guy with the topcoat, comes over, this really elegant guy, he sounds like Alec Guinness in *Lawrence of Arabia*, and he says, "How are you?" and "Why are you here?" and I say, "I'm a writer," and damned if he isn't a writer, too. He's from South Pakistan. Published fourteen novels. He says, "You are not writing now," and I'm getting depressed, and I say, "Why bother?" He smoothes his big gray topcoat, gazes out over the desert, shrugs, and says, "Because life is borink." At the end, the warden comes in and… Oh, skip it. Just ask my brother. That's exactly how it happened, only twenty years ago and the Pakistani was my English teacher and I ran into him in the hall in Parchman Hall.

And we all squeezed into his pickup truck hollerin' and cussin' and wavin' our drumsticks and our sweet cool cans of Dixie beer, shootin' our guns and corruptin' public officials and spittin', just acres of spittin'. That'll work.

Claire

Bailey Long had borrowed five hundred dollars from Claire the month before and so the day he came back to borrow another thousand he was a little touchy. He was standing around in her big white apartment with the dusty hardwood floor looking at what she called "Jersey DNA"—a hunk of chrome in a spiral she had found beside a highway.

"Look," he said, "if you don't want to lend it to me don't lend it to me. Don't do things you don't want to do." He always tried to give some advice while he was sponging, to maintain the advantage he had once had over her.

Claire was sitting at a table by a window, watching him. "Well," she said, "I'm sorry, Bailey, but I just don't have it. I can give you three hundred. But I'll need it all back, say a week? When do you figure to get it back?"

Bailey nodded, casually, trying to affect an air of not caring, taking little fractional steps toward the door of her apartment, fidgeting as if he had business, some place to go. He was a small man, but well-built and good-looking, or had been before he'd gotten middle-aged, which is what he looked now. "Nevermind," he said. "I didn't know you were tapped."

"Don't be silly," she said, and took a pen from a can of pens on the bright windowsill. The can had once held some kind of fancy fruit from Poland or someplace and the label was striking, green, blue, black. Claire had always found things like that, nice things that Bailey overlooked, didn't notice, couldn't

41

see, on his way to some obvious choice, some thing he had read about in a magazine. Her unerring eye, the ease of it, had always been mysterious to him. She shrugged and settled at the long oval table off the kitchen to write out a check. "You need the money. I have the money."

Claire was more beautiful now than she had been in college and in college she had always drawn a crowd. Stop a clock, Bailey thought. Her hair was shorter now and she was given to skirts and loose cream-colored silk blouses instead of T-shirts and jeans but age had made her thin face and her gaudy brown eyes more heart-stopping than they had been, and she wasn't foolish any longer, the way she had had to be foolish to carry on an eleven year love affair with Bailey, living in trashy apartments and making her own clothes and surviving on cheese sandwiches, rice cakes in picante sauce, and beer. Sometimes she seemed like the only thing that had ever happened to him in his whole life.

"Here you go," she said, tearing out the check. "I'd like you to come back tomorrow night, for dinner. I want you to meet my intended. I want to hurt your feelings." She smiled broadly and closed the big checkbook. "How is the store? You a vice president yet?" She stood up and swung her long skirt around her legs as she turned to hand Bailey the check. "Dinner, tomorrow."

"Don't you want to know what I need the money for?"

"Blackjack?" she said, and smiled. "Isn't it? He's just like you. His name is Dave. You'll hate him."

"Dave? I hate him already. Isn't this like stuff people do in movies?"

Her expression went hard. "Exactly. Yes, exactly like that, jerk. But it's the price of your loan." She pointed at the check. "Okay, sweetie? Tomorrow, around eight."

Bailey nodded, leaving. After he had cashed the check, what could she do about it? He'd be all right with this, a little something scrounged off credit cards, maybe a few hundred on the line of credit at the casino, although that made him nervous. They weren't the kind of people you wanted to write bad checks to, really. Start with this, maybe get on a roll, he thought.

When he got to the parking lot in front of the apartments, he saw something move inside his car as he approached it, and his heart started to race. When he got to the car and looked in, a cat, black with blue eyes, was lying on the back seat. What the hell? he thought, and looked around. The parking lot was almost empty. Trees shivered lightly in a gentle wind. He pulled open the rear passenger door. "C'mon," he said. "Get out, stupid."

The black cat, emaciated and hostile looking, sat staring at him, curled on the back seat like a furry black shrimp. Bad luck, Bailey thought.

"C'mon. Get out of the car. C'mon, kitty. I don't know who put you in here, but time to get out." The cat watched him. Bailey reached carefully in over its head and took hold of the scruff of the neck and lifted the cat out of the seat. "Jesus," he said. "You're just bones. You haven't eaten in a month. Easy now." When he carried it to the grass, it curled its back legs up like a kitten. He set it down on the lawn and then stepped backward, away. "Go on," he said, but the cat didn't move, lying the way Bailey had deposited it, head up and tail hidden under its body. It let out a sharp, sudden yowl that sounded like it had just remembered something, an afterthought, and then it blinked.

"Okay," Bailey said. "Just a second."

He shut the back door of the car and opened the front

one, reached in and shook a chocolate bar and a crumpled bag of Cheetos out of a brown paper bag onto the seat. He opened the chocolate bar, broke off a brown corner, and took it to the cat. The cat looked, looked away. "Try it. Here, watch," he said, and took a bite from the bar himself. He nudged the broken off piece closer to the cat, which recoiled slightly, and the chocolate slipped down between blades of grass.

"Twit," Bailey said, and walked back over to his car, finishing the candy bar, glancing back a couple of times. He sighed, and reached in for the Cheetos and uncrumpled the bag. Caught in the bottom were a few scraps of Cheetos, which Bailey emptied onto his palm. He walked back over. The cat yowled again. An old man in wool pants and a brown shirt had come out of his apartment and stood watching them from fifteen feet away.

"Your cat?" Bailey said.

"I like dogs," the old man said. "That looks sick."

Bailey crouched down and opened his hand. The cat jerked forward and cleaned all three Cheetos in one bite. "Hey," Bailey said, and pulled his hand back as the cat tried to lick orange dust from his palm.

"You better get rid of it," the old man standing on his doorstep said. "No pets here."

"It's not mine," Bailey said. He glanced back down the walkway, hoping Claire would come out of her apartment and neutralize this old man somehow.

"You're feeding it," the man said. "Just put it back in your car, boy. Take it to the S.P.C.A., they know what to do with trash animals. Go on."

"Why don't you shut the hell up?" Bailey said. When he looked back down, the cat had slipped away underneath his car. "God damn it."

A blond boy standing on the other side of Bailey's car waved to the old man. "Hey, Mr. Keys, what's going on? Is there a problem?" He looked across at Bailey.

Bailey knelt beside his car. "Shh, go away, I'm stealing a car." He reached under and pulled the cat out.

"This man's trying to ditch his cat here," the old man said.

"Yeah, but Mr. Magoo here caught me," Bailey said, again holding the squirming cat by the scruff of the neck.

"You're kind of sarcastic?" the boy said, coming around the car. He was fair, muscular, wearing an expensive T-shirt and tailored khaki shorts. A weird, hairless looking gray dog walked up as the boy stopped halfway between Bailey and the old man.

The dog sat on its haunches for a millisecond before it saw the cat which had already shaken loose from Bailey's grip. The cat landed upright, looked hastily right and left, and then disappeared backward under the car again while the dog hit the open passenger's door and fell, bounced up again. The dog was snarling, its long fetishy muzzle reaching under the car. "Get this damn dog," Bailey yelled, kicking at it.

"Hey," the boy said. "He won't hurt him." He and the old man were walking over.

"He'll scare the poor little fucker to death, Kato, what're you talking about," Bailey said. He affected a mocking, childish voice: "*He won't hurt him.*"

The dog jumped back, yelling, a weird twisting cry that began in a growl and then raced into something higher pitched and plaintive. It backed away from the side of the car, looking confused, blood all over its face.

The boy was beside it, kneeling down to it, checking the dog's eyes, talking, soothing it with his voice. He looked up at Bailey. "I've got a Magnum in my car," he said. "You better get that fucking cat out of here, cause I'm gonna kill it." The dog started growling again.

"None of that," the old man said, frightened. "None of that now, Davey. You're not supposed to have that dog, you know? I haven't said anything, but—"

"Go inside, Mr. Keys," the boy said, his hand in the dog's collar, restraining it.

"All right," Bailey said. He slammed the passenger door shut and started around the car, then stopped and made a slow sweeping motion with his hand. "All right. Just get the dog away."

The cat, under the far side of the car, lay limp on the blacktop, fast breaths heaving in its gaunt sides, you could see its lungs. Bailey dragged it out as gently as he could, opened the car door and set the cat on the back seat. "Way to go," he whispered, getting into the car.

The blond boy shook his head and sneered. Bailey let the car roll backward out of the parking lot and drove away, thinking he would drop the cat on the next corner, and the next, and the next. But he didn't; he took it home and locked it in his extra bathroom, with an ancient can of tuna fish and a plastic dishpan full of newspaper as a litter box.

• • •

The next day Bailey called in sick at work and went back to sleep until late afternoon. After a shower, he cashed Claire's check at her bank and went by an ATM to squeeze what he could from seven credit cards, then got a soft drink at a drive-through and rolled out of town, headed for the coast casinos with a little over five hundred dollars. He had won sometimes, it wasn't always losing, but even quitting while you were ahead took a discipline that he couldn't seem to maintain once he got inside the places.

Don't eat ice, Bailey told himself, chewing. His teeth were cracked already, lines running up and down every one he looked at when he leaned in close to a mirror, which he did on occasion. It meant you were orally fixated, too, which meant something—you wanted to suck a tit, you were childish, or something. Got that right, Bailey thought. But a quarter of the population smokes cigarettes, which means the same thing supposedly, so it's not so bad, being childish. If you weren't oral, you were anal, was that any better? No way.

He tilted his cup up for more ice. No way, he thought. He had been in the car an hour now, and had another hour's ride. Twilight was rising up ahead of him, orange and dark, reminding him of a place he and Claire had had once, a tiny apartment on one side of a lake with hills on the other side. The apartment had a balcony where they'd sit and watch the sun set behind the hills. One afternoon she said, I bet there's a pile of big orange suns lying around over there somewhere.

Bailey laughed, raised his cup. He would stop in Gulfport, eat a comp steak at that fancy restaurant, then drive down the beach highway to Biloxi. He liked the dealers better there. Maybe I'll make a couple grand and return her money the very next day, he thought. Here, baby, I appreciate the loan. In fact I'm buying you dinner. Bring what's his name.

He had first come down here for a stupid sales education conference that he didn't need, didn't want, and a waste of two weeks of his time and two thousand dollars of the store's money. The "rotunda concept" was what they were big on that year, get the stiffs walking in a circle, merch to the right, merch

47

to the left... Most of the great merchandising concepts were equally sly. He shook his head. The first time he had come down here he had won eight hundred dollars, like it was easy, like it was meant to be. He even won two hundred on a slot machine. Patterson was unhappy when he found out about it, but it had been the old man's idea to send Bailey to the dumb sales conference.

They found out about everything. He remembered when he was hired, how he had been surprised that they knew Claire's name, where she lived, what she did, how long they'd been together. They even knew that girl's name—Dashy—that Bailey was fooling around with when he and Claire split up. "What're y'all running, a department store or the C.I.A.?" he'd said, and none of them had laughed. They actually had a department called "Intelligence." Patterson himself wasn't so bad, just nosy. He paid well, and had done well by Bailey, shooting him up to the second spot in marketing in less than three years, him without even a business degree. Then when they sold the chain to a bigger chain, Patterson had become some kind of token figure, ceased to matter, near as Bailey could tell.

Then he'd started gambling, which was more interesting. It was a department store, who could stay interested in that? It was dull, although he liked the people who worked on the floor, all the clerks and stock people and the tech crew, the people that built displays, moved stuff around. The people who ran the place were horrible, piously stabbing each other for dimes and for the old man's favor. The smart alecks and old drunks at the casinos were far better company. And you never knew, you might make a killing some day, and bye-bye, nine to five. Pay off all the damn bloodsucker credit cards.

He had his free dinner at the steakhouse on top of one of the casinos, and then drove down to Biloxi to another to play.

Two and a half hours later, even betting cautiously and not drinking, he was into his line of credit for a thousand dollars, with about half that left, twenty green chips lined up in front of him.

The dealer was some girl, not anyone he knew, lots of brown hair, very good-looking, looked like a magazine girl, with a magazine girl's indifference. She looked about eighteen but she had two kids, said she was twenty-four. Bailey was thinking about trying another table, when she said, "Press," quietly, and then, when he gave her a doubtful look, reassumed her indifferent expression. She hadn't said more than a dozen sentences in an hour. Bailey stacked the chips, all he had, in one tall stack the way he had seen people do. It was always jerks who did it, but they always won. He pushed the stack onto his spot, and got two face cards and doubled his money. "Black out," she called out for the pit boss, and gave Bailey black hundred dollar chips. He left it all on the spot and doubled it again. And again. And again. She was paying him in purple chips, five hundred dollars apiece. "Wait," Bailey said, and reached out and settled his hand on the chips. The object, he thought, is to get out of this fucking place with some of their money.

The pit boss was standing sort of sideways behind the dealer, watching. Bailey looked up at the girl, who was waiting for his bet, her hand poised over the shoe, her eyes gently blank as if her whole consciousness was pulled back somewhere well behind them. "I don't have the nerves for this," Bailey said. Still nothing.

A Vietnamese man walked up to the table, set some bills down in front of him, looked at Bailey's hand still resting on his chips, then at his face, and picked up the bills and walked away. The pit boss smirked, a chubby guy with stiff permed gray hair and a name tag that said "Lucky." "You're on a roll," he said. "Let it ride." It was a dare, a taunt.

Bailey, sweating, looked at his utterly indifferent dealer again. "Bets," the girl said. Okay, he thought. Once more. He shook his head and stacked all the chips on the round spot on the felt in front of him. "Be nice," he said, and she dealt out the cards. He got a thirteen, an eight and a five, and she dealt herself a deuce. She looked at him.

"Dealer's ace," Lucky said. "Glad that's not my eight grand." He laughed, and glanced away, over at each of the other tables in the pit, as if this game were already over. "She could still break," Lucky said, doubtfully, and laughed again.

Just a stupid thing everybody says about deuces, Bailey thought, but he didn't like that the pit boss had counted his chips, or counted them so accurately. Or maybe they had it fixed. Players' paranoia, he thought. Can't mean anything. The dealer was waiting for him to play. Not this, he thought, shaking his head. It's twelve against a three you're supposed to hit. But he tapped the felt with his index finger twice, asking for a hit. She laid down a card, a three, now he had sixteen. The pit boss rocked, smirking. Bailey lifted his hands in a gesture of surrender, took a breath, rocking, too, a little, forward and back, he couldn't stop the movement. "I'm good," he said, and waved his hand flat above his cards. "I'll stay. Turn it up."

She turned up her down card, a queen, spades.

"That's a start," the pit boss said. "That's a good start."

The girl dealt herself another card, a deuce, and then a third deuce. It was taking forever. "Sixteen," she said, and stopped, and a hint of a smile slipped over her face. Why wasn't she dealing it? Bailey thought. Do it. "Twenty-six?" she said, and flipped out another card, another queen.

"Twenty-six," Bailey said, breathing out, and he shook his

50

head sharply as he felt tears rising in his eyes. "It's twenty-six. Dealer busts."

"Misdeal," Lucky shouted. And then, when he saw the look on Bailey's face, "Little jokie." And then he wandered away to a telephone and a computer at a stand in the middle of the pit.

"Color these up," Bailey said, pushing his chips toward the dealer. "I can't—" He shrugged. "—do this."

He watched, wondering if he had figured it right, trying to recount his stacks himself as she counted up his chips and made stacks from hers, all purples, sixteen thousand dollars. Lucky was back, watching. "Sixteen thousand," the girl said.

"Sixteen thousand," Lucky said. "Okay."

When she had pushed the chips across to Bailey, he took one and slid it across the insurance line to her and slipped the rest of them into his shirt pocket. "Thank you, ma'am," he said. His hands were shaking.

The girl took it blankly. "Thank you, sir," she said, then called out, "Dropping five hundred for the dealers, for the boys and girls," and slipped the chip into the toke box by her right hand. The dealers at the other tables turned to look.

Get out, Bailey thought, checking his pocket. Cash it all in. Don't look at the slots. Don't think. Walk to the cashier, he thought, and headed that way. At the main cage he asked for twelve thousand in a check and the rest in cash. The I.R.S. would hear, anything over ten. It only took a few minutes, but getting the chips cashed in felt like landing an airliner. He looked this way and that. Suddenly all the casino patrons looked like sleazy bit actors on *NYPD Blue*.

It wasn't until he was in the car on the highway with the dark pine trees and bare fields passing by outside that he began to breathe easy again, and even then he kept patting his pocket for the fold of hundreds and the twelve thousand dollar check they'd given him. And then he started laughing, quietly, to himself, but that made him self-conscious so he just shook his head a little.

He drove straight to Claire's, but he didn't get there until after midnight, and the windows of her apartment were all dark. Then he remembered the dinner he had been supposed to come to. Whoops, he thought. Well, I never said I'd be there. I'll take her to dinner tomorrow, he thought. Take some roses, too. *Really* piss her off. So he pulled out of the parking lot and drove back to his own apartment.

He had completely forgotten the cat, which started yowling the moment his key went in the door lock and didn't let up until he opened the bathroom door. "Jesus," Bailey said, "shut up. You aren't winning any friends that way."

The cat sat on the edge of the bathtub, looking up.

Bailey let it follow him into the kitchen where he shuffled through the cabinets looking for something to feed it. "Looks like you're out of luck, Slick," he said. "That was my only can of tuna fish." He took down a plastic bag of chocolate chip cookies and ripped it open.

"Here," he said, and dropped a cookie on the linoleum in front of the cat, which looked at it. "Moist and chewy," Bailey said. "And don't give me any twaddle about this, as until yesterday you've been eating out of the garbage unless I miss my guess. I'll get some Cheetos tomorrow." He dropped another cookie beside the first one, and the cat set himself down to dinner. "That's better," Bailey said.

He went into the living room and lay back in the big chair, watching the kitchen doorway, waiting for the cat to come in and start hassling him again. He turned on the TV, but left the sound muted, and thought about the money that was still in his shirt pocket, touching it every once in a while. It came to him that Claire wouldn't care about it, not at all. She'd be happy to take her loan money back, but that's all. He hadn't done anything at all, the way she saw it. Just didn't matter to her. He ran through some channels on the TV, settled on some talk show, set the control down. He touched his pocket, looked toward the kitchen. "Goddamn it," he said, "get in here, you pest."

• • •

It was a little after four in the morning when he went out and got in his car and started back over to Claire's apartment. He wasn't drunk. He'd had a couple beers to try to mellow out, but it hadn't worked. There was no way he was going to be able to sleep with all that brand new money. There was something disappointing about it, anyway. It was like being a kid and doing something really spectacular about which no one cared, like getting all the way home through the woods without ever touching the ground, or hitting a home run in an empty ballpark, when it didn't count.

Maybe they could try again, him and Claire. He didn't feel about new women the way he had felt about her, that it mattered, that it could end well, that it might not end. You met a woman and even if you had more than fifteen minutes worth of talk in common, even if she could say something interesting or funny, you were thinking, when do we find out what's wrong with her, what's wrong with me that she can't tolerate, how long before we find out. But he didn't feel about Claire the way he felt about them, either, that weird sort of hunger for them, for their faces, for their eyes. Claire's eyes were beautiful but it wasn't the same. You know me, you don't know me, look, don't look, don't look away.

The place was all dark when Bailey got there, and he sat in his car out front, trying to think of a way to put it, something to say to her, looking at the still, sleeping apartment building. But what did he want to say? The small lights in glass at the corners of the building, marking the ends of the three walkways into the interior courtyard, seemed friendly, almost like living things. He turned the key partway in the ignition to get the dashboard clock to light. 4:24. This is not normal behavior, he thought. This is the way I used to behave, before I got a job. Marketing.

On the concrete walk, he stepped as lightly as he could, making his way into the courtyard and then past a half dozen doors to hers. His knock was stuttering, and waiting, he glanced quickly up and back the walk, afraid to see a light come on in some other apartment. Claire's door swung open a few inches, and she stood blinking her brown eyes at him, holding her shoulders. Air conditioning floated out around her.

"You're late, Bailey," she said, and frowned. "You're way late." She was dressed in an aluminum colored negligee edged with lace, and floppy white socks. She was wearing her glasses, and Bailey felt suddenly as if he had accidentally touched her, bumped into her. It seemed unfair that he was so close to her and she should look like this, like she had a life, preoccupied. It wasn't what he had expected, although he hadn't really expected anything. But it was as if they had agreed ever since their final separation to meet in a certain way, relaxed, not formal, but not en dishabille either, not personal.

"For dinner, I mean," she said. "I was asleep."

"I brought your money back," Bailey said. "All of it." It

sounded pathetic, but everything else he could think of seemed wrong.

She began to laugh, sleepily, and then nodded, more to herself than to him, and opened the door. There was a gray dog standing beside her. The apartment's white walls looked faintly yellow in the moonlight. "By all means, then," she said. "Come in."

Bailey stood staring at the dog, the same dog from yesterday afternoon, or its twin brother. He was shaking his head, trying to sort it out, trying to separate the scene in the parking lot and Claire, Claire and the dog, four o'clock in the morning and—

"Come in," she said again, emphatically. Behind her, standing in the tiny hall at the doors to the apartment's bathroom and bedrooms, was the boy who owned the dog. He was holding a pair of slacks in one hand, barefoot on the wood floor, wearing boxer shorts and brushing his hundred dollar haircut back with his hand, looking at Bailey, who didn't really know what to do.

Bailey stepped inside and the air conditioning hit him full force. The dog loped back to the blond boy. The boy put his pants on.

Claire, having added a pale blue oxford shirt, tried to shake off Bailey's stare, looked away, looked back, then again, the same gesture, and failing, started talking.

"Oh stop. It's the middle of the night and you have come to my place ostensibly to return some money at—" She checked the clock on the microwave on the kitchen counter, squinting. "—at four forty-five a.m., which is not really banking hours, you know, after failing to appear at a dinner at which you agreed to appear and which was bought and cooked as per agreement, if you know what I mean. So stop fucking staring at me."

"I think you'd just better go," the boy said.

"Dave," Claire said, and shot a glance at him.

"Okay," he said.

"This is Bailey Long," she said. "My old flame. Love of my former life. Bailey, Dave Boyette, my fiancé." She slid up on a barstool beside the counter.

"Hi," Bailey said, and then to Claire, "We ran into each other yesterday." *Davey*, he thought, still trying to assemble the pieces of the situation into something coherent. The old man called him "Davey." "Somebody put a cat in my car," he said, and then he thought, She won't get that, that doesn't make any sense at all. "It's a long story," he said. "This kid carries a gun, did you know that? It's in his car? It's one thing to hang around with teenagers, but *armed* teenagers?"

"Look—" Dave began, but this time Claire only had to look at him. He sighed. "Okay," he said.

"Bailey, this is Dave Boyette. My fiancé," she said, and wiggled her toes in her sock, pointing. "The one I told you about."

"Yeah, but I didn't take you seriously," Bailey said.

"You probably should have," the boy said, advancing into the front room for the first time, passing between Bailey and Claire and walking around the counter into the kitchen, taking a new tack. "Do you want a beer or something? Pepsi?" His dog came with him, shy of Bailey, settling on a throw rug near Claire's feet.

She slid off the bar stool. "Well, if we're going to have... conversation," she said, "I'll feel more comfortable with some clothes on. I'll be a minute. You boys can start over, how about?" she said, and walked back into the bedroom.

"She's a great lady," Dave said, breaking the silence. "You want something?"

"Beer. A beer," Bailey said. He sat at the table off the

kitchen by the front window and took the money out of his shirt pocket, set the roll in front of him and counted off eight hundred dollar bills, his debt. "Listen, I'm sorry about the other afternoon. It really wasn't my cat."

"So you're the big gambler," Dave said. He handed a bottle over to Bailey and took a chair across from him. "I go down there sometimes."

"No, I'm a department store salesman who plays too much blackjack," Bailey said, looking around for Claire.

"What's all that?"

"Money," Bailey said.

"I could tell that much." Dave sat back in his chair. "You're making this harder than it has to be, you know? I'm trying to get along, and I really don't have any reason to."

Bailey settled his head in his hand and shook it gently. This must be what it comes to, he thought. Sitting here sick at your stomach, getting advice about life from a teenager. This is how you pay for rank stupidity, for slovenliness, for falling a little short at everything your whole life long.

He looked across at Dave. "Sorry. I didn't mean to be making it hard. That's money I owe Claire, some of it is, which I am paying her back, which she lent me." He looked over his shoulder toward the back of the apartment. "Sorry I woke you up. When it is you're getting married?"

"December," Dave said. "I wanted to do it right away, but Claire wanted to wait. Her parents are in Fort Worth—but I guess you know them."

Bailey nodded. He heard a whistle from outside the window, and then again. That's a bird, he thought. That's morning. He looked toward the window, but the sky hadn't begun to light. "What do you do for a living, Dave?"

"Now you sound like her parents," the boy said. "I'm

second year at the law school. I was managing Bechtold's— the restaurant—but you know, I needed to make—" Bailey looked up, then followed the boy's glance to Claire, who had apparently been watching. "That's better," she said. Now she was wearing white jeans and a shirt of her own, white, a short sleeveless tunic.

"A Snapple?" Dave said, standing and reaching for the refrigerator door. She smiled, his answer.

Bailey looked at the table in front of him. "I guess I'll go," he said. "Sorry to barge in, I don't know what I was doing. No, I know what I was doing. I just won sixteen grand and I had to tell somebody, I guess." He picked up his money and stuffed it into his pocket. "Here's the eight I owe you," he said and handed Claire the hundreds he had taken from the roll.

She took the money and kissed him, laughing. "You really won sixteen thousand dollars? That's great, Bailey. Aren't you happy? You're going to quit now, I hope?"

Dave let the refrigerator door fall closed and handed her a bottle of what looked like pink lemonade. "Jesus," he said. "That's a lot of money."

"Bailey?" Claire said.

"I gotta go," he said, and nodded to Dave. "It was good to meet you."

Dave stood to shake hands. The dog got to its feet. "Good to meet you," Dave said.

"I'll walk you out?" Claire said. She took a drink of lemonade and set the bottle on the table beside the hundreds, but then thought better of it and picked the bottle up again and walked out the door, leaving Bailey and the boy standing there.

"Good night," Bailey said and turned and followed Claire outside.

He found her sitting with her lemonade beside her on a

low concrete wall at the edge of the property, near where his car was parked. It was still not quite morning, although the air was wet and birds were already chirping and whistling all around.

"I wanted to show you all this dumb money," Bailey said, taking it out of his pocket in a ball, staring at it. "Isn't that pathetic?" He settled beside her on the concrete wall, shaking his head slowly back and forth. "You're busy doing the watata with the sweetheart of Sigma Chi." He shrugged. "Sorry. I didn't mean that." He threw the money on the grass.

Claire laughed. "And you accuse *me* of making movie gestures?" she said, and slipped off the wall.

"Okay," Bailey said, "right. Give me that back. Make sure the ink isn't running on that damn check."

She handed him the dewy money, yawning.

"All the good gestures have been gestured," he said, replacing it in his shirt pocket. "So, I mean, what are you thinking? Breeding stock? It's not only that he's not me, he's not even *like* me."

"You'd like that better?" Claire said, sipping lemonade. The glass bottle clanked when she set it back down on the wall.

"No, I guess not. But he has a dog. He has a gun. He's a goddamn norm. He's the enemy."

"He wants to have children."

"Oh, Jesus, it *is* breeding stock." Bailey caressed the concrete wall absentmindedly, then realizing it, lifted his hand to touch his forehead with the tips of his fingers, then clapped his hand on his jeans above the knee. "Look, marry me. We'll have children, tomorrow, or Friday. I'd like to have children. Can we use a Skinner box? We have these gahunga cat carriers for dogs at the store—perfect for children. Claire?"

She was watching a police car cruising up the street and

past the apartments. The cop, a kid wearing sunglasses even though it had barely gotten light, gave them his best stare as he passed. "Only you are good enough for me, is that it?" she said.

Bailey's heart sank a little. That was it. It occurred to him for the first time that maybe it wasn't true, or that maybe the whole notion of "good enough" didn't have anything to do with it. "No," he said, weakly. "Don't be silly."

"We're in love," Claire said. "Whether we meet your specifications or not."

"I got a new cat," Bailey said. "Somebody here put it in my car Monday while I was talking to you. When I came out, it was in the car. I tried to leave it here. Then your precious boyfriend drove up and offered to blow it away with his big pistola. I guess he's a dog person." He feigned a smile. "I keep trying to figure out when my life ended. It wasn't when we split up, it was before that. It was when I got that goddamn job, I think. I just didn't notice because the job itself was distracting. Anything can be interesting for a while. And then you dumped me. It's like, this money, this sixteen grand? I stopped caring about it ten minutes out of Biloxi. What good is it? I can pay off credit cards."

"You had another girl," Claire said. "Did you forget? She was about twenty and very tall, if I remember correctly." She laughed, then stopped as abruptly as she had started and rubbed her chin, a weird, mannish gesture. "I remember every damn thing about her. She had a stupid name. Dashy. One of her charms, I guess."

"You don't feel like your life ended? Really? I don't mean when we split up." Bailey looked at her, looked away. "Like what you're doing now is just so much busy work?"

In her white outfit, in the soft morning light, she didn't

60

look so much uncomprehending as horribly indifferent. She shrugged. "I got older."

Bailey stood up. "All that time, the time when we were together, when I was a lowlife, a slacker, every goddamn day, it was electric. Something wonderful was coming. I remember how wonderful stuff at the grocery store was, those Rubbermaid things and the little hardware display and funny vegetables. Then I got a job and a nice fat salary." He turned his palms up and gave her a puzzled look. "All gone," he said.

"Bailey, I don't—"

"No," he said sharply, suddenly afraid. "Nevermind. Sorry to bother you with this rot." He smiled, a quick fake. Who knows what she might have been about to say, he thought. It was okay that she was intending to marry some perfectly ordinary young blond boy and go off to believe with him in everything that in the past they together they had not believed in. It was even okay to no longer believe in the things that they had believed in together. But he didn't want to hear that it had never happened, that he had understood it wrong, that he had in fact been alone then, too. The idea of it made him shudder. She put her arm around him, leaning in, as if to kiss him, and hesitated. "Bailey?"

"Anyway, this cat is skinny," he said, "looks like he hasn't eaten since the Bicentennial. You'll come see him sometime. He's black, looks a little like Otto." He glanced vaguely out into the damp morning air, closed his eyes, and shuddered again. "Still like cats, don't you?" he said, waiting, urgently, for her kiss.

That Story about Freddy Hylo

I had been gambling for more than 36 hours, begged off work the next day, called my wife and told her I wouldn't be back until tomorrow, hadn't slept and hadn't eaten and was about out of money when Richie called me and told me he was coming to meet me at the casino. I was almost at the point where you can't remember the rules of blackjack, where you have to play standing up, where you look at your cards and you're trying to remember what the object of the game is, and how to add. I may have been seeing things, too, a little, corner of the eye stuff that wasn't there, that sort of thing.

Richie brought a friend, a little guy named Freddy Hylo, pronounced High-Low. They showed up around midnight. It gave me the creeps because the only time I had ever heard that name, it was in a story I heard when I was a kid, a story about a guy busting out another guy's teeth by breaking them on a piece of sandstone in his mouth. And this guy was scary. I'm six-one, 195, and he couldn't have been more than about five-nine, but he was sort of terrifying. I don't know what it was, something in his face, his eyes, you looked at him and thought, this is a guy that doesn't care about *anything*.

We wandered around the casino for about four hours, playing table games, sitting in one of the clubs where the band was actually pretty good, hitting on the girls who looked like teenagers, without a lot of luck. By about three in the morning, Richie had found himself this blonde girl in a tiny gray dress that looked like it was made out of microfiber dust cloths. I had thought she was a professional, but what do I know? I was at a blackjack table with Hylo and two other people, some drunk asshole in a leather jacket and a Vietnamese woman, who were exchanging looks when we played, complaining when Hylo hit a 12 against a dealer's 2, a standard by-the-book draw. "Took her bust card," the asshole would say, and the woman would agree almost imperceptibly. Hylo didn't react, it was like he didn't even hear.

Richie came up behind us holding the blonde, bent over to me. "I got a room." He pointed toward the ceiling. "In the hotel," he said, and glanced at the girl.

"No, Jesus, don't leave me with this guy," I said, as quietly as I knew how. "C'mon, Rich." But he was already walking away with her, her wispy dress swinging back and forth.

The drunk guy in the leather jacket was looking at me. "You gonna bet, champ?"

I shoved a couple of greens onto my spot.

After me, Hylo put out ten dollars, two reds.

"High roller," the drunk guy said. "Be a man, man." He was betting a hundred a hand, winning most of them. The rest of us were above water, but that's all.

· · ·

I was driving the car and Hylo had the asshole in the backseat and was instructing him in etiquette with a razor. I didn't want him in my car, but they must have come in Richie's. Richie and the blonde girl were long gone. I could see the attraction. I wouldn't have been in the car with Freddy, in fact I never would have been anywhere with Freddy if I could've avoided it, but I hadn't been able to get out of it when he asked me to drive. He was not really asking, exactly.

"Pull it over," he said.

"You want a Whataburger?"

"Yeah, I want a Whataburger. You want a Whataburger, champ?" he said to his companion in the backseat. The guy, who had been giving us shit at a blackjack table, had disappeared and then later, when we stopped in the last men's room before the parking garage, he had walked into the men's room and said something to Freddy about the long coat he had on, something suggesting Freddy was a flasher. Freddy said, "You're some kind of expert in that area?" and then out came the razor, and here we are now, behind the Whataburger, dazzlingly bright lights around the restaurant, some kind of service road in front of us, a strip center, dark, behind us.

The parking lot was empty, but I parked to the side and toward the back and got out of the Citroen and turned toward the Whataburger. We were beside what looked in the dark like five thousand dollars' worth of pointless landscaping, a Japanese garden with sand and pebbles, stone and sago palms. There was nobody in the place, near as I could see. "Open 24 Hours" was painted on the window, in orange and white. Everything was orange and white. It was four in the morning.

"Hey," Freddy said, standing on the other side of the car. "Where you goin'?"

"Hamburger," I said. "Right?"

Freddy shook his head. "Stay here. Keep an eye out."

"Freddy, let the asshole go. Let's eat."

He gave me a look. "Wouldn't be right," he said.

At that point the other guy took a half hearted swing at him and Freddy turned and knocked him backward about three feet, handed me the razor, and then hit him three or four more times, very fast, with his fists and his elbow, and the guy went down. On the ground, the guy was whimpering. All the fight gone out of him in two seconds—it was bizarre. Freddy had his hair in his hand, and with his other arm reached out toward me. "Give me the knife," he said.

I looked at him. My hands were shaking. "Fuck no, what're you, crazy? Let him go."

"Give me the knife."

I handed it to him.

I thought, Oh, fuck, and looked quickly into the restaurant and then up and down the street. There was nobody. When I turned back around, Freddy was shoving a flat piece of sandstone from the landscaping into the guy's mouth, and then he raised his boot way up and brought it down on the guy's head. Teeth or something scattered around Freddy's feet. I stood staring at the pristine, almost fastidious little garden with its squat palms inside a perfect rim and then the blood on the concrete and blood all around the guy's mouth. Freddy flipped the razor open and whacked a hunk of the guy's hair off, looked at it and stretched, slipped it into his pants pocket. This seemed to satisfy him and he let the guy's head hit the pavement and looked at me.

I didn't know what to do. He waved toward the restaurant, asking, then turned back around and kicked the moaning guy on the concrete again.

"I'm not hungry," I said. "Let's go."

"No, I'm hungry." He stared at me. Behind him, the guy got up and sort of half ran, half crawled away toward the dark shops of the strip center. Hylo laughed.

• • •

Everything in the place was weird orange and white stripes. I kept waiting for cops to show up but they never did. Freddy was eating onion rings. He had asked for two orders of them, but the black kid who brought the food to the table brought three. The kid stood, with an orange plastic tray on a strap around his neck, like a cigarette girl, approving. When he put the stuff down in front of us, he said, "These are so good… I just really love these onion rings."

"They're good all right," Freddy said.

The kid was maybe seventeen and there was about him this huge, terrible sweetness and you looked at him and thought, This poor kid is just gonna get crushed. He took his tray and walked back to the counter, behind it, and disappeared.

Now Hylo was talking to me. "What did you learn to-night?" He smiled.

"Don't be an asshole?"

"Exactly," he said, smiled, looked around. "You don't like me much, do you?"

I just caught what he said. I was shaking, my whole body trembling, just a little. "This can't be," I said. "It's not… It can't be. I heard this story twenty-five years ago, when I was twelve. The stone in the guy's mouth, the whole thing. The reason I know it can't be is that— In the story, the guy's name was Hylo."

He was eating. He didn't seem to hear me, but then he shrugged. "When you heard that story, who did you imagine yourself to be?"

"What do you mean?"

"Did you imagine yourself to be the guy smashing the

67

other guy's teeth, or did you imagine yourself to be the guy getting a limestone sandwich?"

I looked at him. I had the car keys in my hand.

"That's really all there is," he said. He was looking out the big plate glass windows, in a weary sort of way, at the bright, clean parking lot. The restaurant was new, looked sort of like Alphaville. "You go on. I'll get a cab."

I looked around the place for someone else, but there was nobody anywhere, just, out there, the empty 4 a.m. streets and the lights and a stupid stoplight pointlessly changing colors, red to green. Outside I got into the car and glanced back through the restaurant windows half expecting Hylo to be gone, turned to vapor. But he was still in there.

Telephone

It'll be like this. The phone will ring, at some wrong time, some time the phone never rings, six o'clock in the evening or four a.m., or noon. It's Ben, my brother. Ben always knows everything first, makes it his business to know things, so it'll be him. How is he going to sound? Cool? Weeping? That high-serious voice he gets whenever something terrible happens? No, that voice isn't for truly terrible things, but for those things we treat as terrible, talisman to protect us from the really terrible. The phone rings, it's Ben. "Tommy," he says, "I just got a call from Baltimore. It's Pop—"

No, that's not it. It'll be a message on the answering machine, the rectangular red light blinking when I go into the kitchen in the morning, and I'll see it and I'll think it's something else, someone I want to hear from, something maybe I want to hear, something that I've been waiting for, something good. It'll be Ben, of course, leaving a message. The message will say, "Pop died this morning at—" and then there'll be some time, he'll say "5:55 a.m." the way people do, as if it made any difference. It'll be some picturesque time, like 5:55 a.m., some time which stays in your brain forever after, not a time you can forget.

Then the message will continue, Ben sounding like a cop. "Call me. I'm flying over there this afternoon, and if I haven't heard from you, I'll call you when I get there. Mom is okay, just crazy. Laura is taking care of her, she's at Laura's house.

That number is—well, you have Laura's number..." Then the message will change, his voice will change, he'll say, "I didn't know this was going to be this way, I didn't know..." and he won't be able to finish the thought. "Call me," he'll say.

I am standing in the kitchen, listening to my brother on the answering machine. I'm half awake. I don't feel anything. I have to wait for some place where I'm safe enough to feel something. I have been waiting for this message for twenty-five years, since my father was about sixty. This is what it'll be like. Twenty-five years of waiting wasted. This is it. What is it like? Standing in my kitchen. I will punch the rewind and play the message again. "...at 5:55 a.m.," my brother says. "I didn't know this was going to be this way," he says. It's over, I will think. As a child, when my mother wasn't home, I used to listen to sirens, stand looking out the big windows of the front room, looking into the empty carport, waiting for her car to be back in its place, and it always came back.

As a child, I got to play chess with him. He would lie on his elbow on the kingsize bed and I would sit on a low stool, the wooden chessboard on another stool between us. Sometimes he was in pajamas. Maybe he was letting me win, those times I won. Now, middle-aged, I remember things he said, advice, some of it. He did not say, It's bad and then it gets worse. Once he took one of his records, with "Unbreakable" printed on the label, and bent the record in half until it broke. "Not unbreakable," he said, and then he laughed. What kind of person would do that? I think. I like to think that twenty-five years anticipating has immunized me against emptiness, but it isn't so.

I wanted my father to be all the things that an ideal man is supposed to be, a hero. He wasn't far off the mark, really. He got worse as I got older, but my idea of what a hero was incorporated worse things, too. And it kept things orderly for him to be a hero. He has been a stranger to me since I was about twenty-five, twenty years.

The telephone will ring, it'll be the message, this is how it will feel, I can imagine it. I will feel like an animal standing at the margin of a field beside a fence, head high as if catching a new, totally unknown scent, afraid but not terrified, confused but not bewildered, hurts to swallow, feeling all the muscles in my jaw, in my arms, unable to run, not wanting to run, hearing my heartbeat. I will do what I'm supposed to, walk, talk, a suit. I can imagine it.

Bye Bye Brewster

For two years or so I had enjoyed thinking of myself as a great friend to Brewster until the day I understood that I was not, a day shortly before he moved out of the apartment complex we both lived in. I had managed to forget that day until yesterday morning when his daughter called—he'd mentioned a daughter somewhere in the east—and told me Brewster had died the day before. I was shaken, it couldn't be. But of course it was.

She was in town, from Connecticut, for a few more days. She had been with him when he died. He'd left me some money. I was to take one of his cats, too, she said, he said you'd know which one. Could I come over to the house? Did I know where it was? She gave me the address, and I agreed to drop by later in the day. She said, "I don't know what to do with the other cats; there're so many." I knew which one; we had had a stupid quarrel over it once, but that had gotten straightened out. Still, I didn't bother going over there, the afternoon passed and I had dinner and watched something on HBO and by that time it seemed awful late. I didn't need a cat to take care of, anyway.

I hadn't seen Brewster since he moved, about five months ago. It was eerie, imagining him speaking—about me—yesterday or the day before and now not speaking anymore. He was twice my age, but a bond had been fashioned out of necessity, because he was old and alone, because my life had turned up all zeroes—all I had was a job and this apartment. It hasn't gotten any better since he moved. It seems sort of strange, but the time I knew him had become in my memory an oddly contented and happy time, one of those periods of one's life during which one bitches and complains incessantly which later in retrospect becomes a life sorely missed. There wasn't anything extraordinary about those months: we had shared a lot of evenings, eaten together, played card games, talked a lot, did some drinking, awaited and then watched favorite TV shows every week, rituals of a friendship. He had lent me money and then forgiven the debts; I had helped him out sometimes. He said his son was in California, maybe Washington state. He never heard from him. I had had a father who was easy to disappoint, and after I disappointed him I took poor care of him, which maybe explains the Brewster thing.

For the two years we were friends I did everything that Brewster needed done, so much so that I got into the habit of knocking on his door when I got home from work in case there was some errand or muscle work he needed, so I could get it done before I settled in to watch the news and have dinner, so that I wouldn't be interrupted; it was a practical matter. I would walk up an extra flight of the steel and concrete stairs at the apartments, past mine on the second level, up to his on the third, knock and wait until he came to the door, say Hi, as if I were checking on him.

Often he didn't have anything for me to do. But sometimes he'd have some job he'd saved all day until I got home, hold this, drill this, cut this, move these over there and those where these were, do you know where I can find a good this, maybe you could accompany me there. He had been an engineer but his father had done millwork and fine carpentry, worked a lathe, skills Brewster had learned as a boy and used to make tables and shelving, cabinets, and small cases for things, beautifully crafted boxes made from wood and covered in fabric, although now at seventy-something his hands were unsteady and his eyes were shot.

One month I took him to the eyeglasses place six times on lunch hours and hours out from work, trying to get him a pair of glasses through which he could see. I never knew, still don't know, whether the glasses were good and he was just crazy or whether the optometrists and opticians were the most incompetent fools God ever made. It was funny, watching them try to deal with him, condescending but forgiving him everything because he was old, him playing that for all it was worth. We'd laugh afterward, but each time he would say, "I really can't see worth a damn," no matter how many times they remade the glasses. "They just think I'm a crazy old duck," he would say.

"An old duck" is what he called himself and any other old man he liked. A man he didn't like was a "louse." I liked him, in part, because he talked like no one else I knew, probably only a reflection of his age, vestiges of another time showing in his vocabulary, favorite expressions, a reserve or restraint which prevented him from using vulgar language, though "damn" and "hell" were common coin.

I still live in the apartment complex. He had been here for years—I never was clear on how many—when I moved in two years ago. I don't want to go to his place. I don't want to see it. When he was evicted from the apartments, he asked me to move with him, to split the house he was moving to. I had sort of agreed, at least we had talked about getting a place at one time, so he had reason to expect it, but when it really came up, I couldn't get over the idea of moving in with a seventy year old man. He was way past caring about how strange such a roommate arrangement might seem. I was also afraid of getting still more tangled up than I already was, of his growing dependency, of making my temporary abandonment of social life with people of my own age and station into a permanent condition.

Splitting a house with Brewster might not have meant that, but at the time the prospect felt like being pulled under water I had been just sort of pleasantly floating in, expecting sometime sooner or later to return to land. So I guess I wasn't much of a friend to him, when it came down to it, or at least had misrepresented the friend I was.

"You know," Brewster said, "you could move in with me. Take half the house. There're two kitchens over there. Four bedrooms." We were standing on the concrete walkway outside the apartment he was leaving. He was serious. "We could split it up any way you want." His body was short and heavy with a belly and thick forearms, still strong. His big, bald, ruddy face had round areas where the skin looked thin and stretched, broken capillaries, spots, and some kind of ugly black scar or growth on one ear. He was looking at me. I should say something, I thought, but the only thing in my head was what I usually said to Brewster—"Sure"—and I didn't want to say that. Finally I said, "Well," and looked down into the courtyard, so obviously with nothing to look at that I almost stumbled into the railing. Brewster shrugged, and the light left his blue eyes. "Well, you can think about it," he said. "House isn't going anywhere." He nodded to the door of his now bare apartment. "Play some cards?" We went in.

• • •

They had no reason to throw him out, but they said it was the cats. Brewster had nine cats, and two of them lived in the stove, an ordinary sort of eccentricity, as common as cornflakes, the kind of thing nobody gives a moment's thought until for some other reason the light of the community shines on you and suddenly there's a mob of good upstanding citizens all jabbering fiercely to each other. The place smelled, of course, even though the cats were pretty good about it, they would do their business outside under the shrubbery or on the tiny lawn around the apartments. Every night at ten o'clock, the old man's door would swing open ten inches or so and the cats, or most of them, would step out single file—a big old Siamese, followed by a gray, two black ones, a fluffy calico, another that looked red, others. They'd step along the walk and down the concrete stairway like ducks, and then scatter, and if they didn't all come back smartly at ten thirty, you would hear the old man whistling for the stragglers.

I had met Brewster a few weeks after I had taken the apartment on the floor below him. It's a four-story building with forty or forty-five apartments, a large parking area at one end. One sunny Saturday afternoon I was working on my car in the parking lot, a simple repair, putting new pads in the brakes, and he came out and lent me a hand. Car repair was clearly not considered proper parking lot activity at this complex, which added to Brewster's pleasure in helping out. We got along well from the first. It wasn't long before we joked about getting a place together somewhere, about getting away from the old women who more or less ran our building. He was chary of the management company, too, because of the cats.

He was particularly sweet on the Siamese, whose name was Antibody, but he called it "A. B.," or more often, "Abe." It was about sixteen years old, and liked its comforts. The one I liked best was what they call a "snowshoe," a cat that looked Siamese-y but with bright white paws and nose, like the "points" were reversed. This one, the one we argued about, Brewster called "Killer-T." It was some kind of weird joke. He spent contented hours reading medical magazines at a branch library.

The first time I saw one of the cats wander into the kitchen and jump onto the open door of the oven and walk into it, I stopped what we were doing—we were playing gin—and pointed and stuttered, "The cat, the cat," but he just smiled and nodded and told me they lived in there, the twin black ones. All the cats except for the one he called Red had names out of the P.D.R.—the *Physicians Desk Reference,* which I soon discovered was probably Brewster's favorite book—christened after disease fighters, cells and medicines—Leukocyte and Lymphocat, Amoxicillin and Streptomycin, and so on. The old man was a hypochondriac as well as a cat lover, and although it was an ironic hypochondria, he wasn't joking. He didn't like doctors much, but when I took him to see them, he repeated what they said as if it were the revealed word of God. His refrigerator was crowded with carrots and brussels sprouts and broccoli, wheat germ, tofu and tuna fish, DHEA, glucosamine and other pills, as well as jars of olive oil, which looked like green lard.

We spent a lot of time playing games. I work for the city in the Clerk Assessor's office, I'm twice divorced, and my mother and sister live over a thousand miles from here in Arizona, so I guess I needed Brewster as much as he needed me. I spent a lot of evenings up there playing gin, blackjack, whist, even Hold 'em, as well as Scrabble and checkers and chess. For a month or so once we played a basketball game we made up, best of ten shots, using a plastic bucket and a ball he'd bought at the supermarket. We even went to a bar one time and shot pool for a couple of hours, but he didn't care for the atmosphere. It depressed him—"too much smoke and too many young women with too little clothes on," he said. I think he just didn't like losing.

The cats were outlaws. Our leases prohibited pets, but lots of people kept them, and no one ever hassled any of us about it. It's benign neglect. Once a week or so now, whenever I get in the service elevator to go down to the washers and dryers in the basement, there's some ditzy guy with a couple of big fluffy spaniels or whatever they are, heading out for their walk.

I had taken to letting Snowshoe into my apartment, but it was when she started spending the night at my place that Brewster got upset and threatened getting me evicted. I told him that "Killer" was a stupid name for a cat that was as sweet and lamblike as it could be. He made fun of me for saying "lamblike" and said I didn't know what I was talking about. He said he was going to call the damn police on me if I ever did it again. Astonished, I told him the cat never wanted to leave, and I wasn't going to force the cat out the door if it didn't want to go. He said just remember what he'd told me. I'd be looking for a new apartment in the time it took to say "Jack Robinson." "Jack Robinson," I said. We were behaving like children.

That was in August, when everyone was in a foul mood because of the heat. We had window unit air-conditioners which were old and noisy and expensive to run, so you either stayed in the cool part of the apartment all the time or you went out. Brewster was smart; he spent the hot afternoons at the library, where they had the AC cranked up to flurries. The cat, Snowshoe, as soon as Brewster let them out in the morning, came down to sit outside my front window. Brewster's other cats hung around together and when any of the neighbors' cats got aggressive, two or three of Brewster's would start showing shoulders and snarling, and if that weren't enough they'd cut the other one up. Sometimes there were complaints, but mostly it was only noise and mostly he got them inside by ten-thirty, so it was never a big problem.

By late in August Brewster and I had sort of patched things up—I gave in, is how that went. I liked playing cards, especially when my only likely alternative was an evening flipping through my forty-eight channels on the remote control and then going to bed tired but not sleepy.

I wasn't dating then, hadn't been since I got my second divorce, which wasn't an actual divorce because Michelle and I had just been keeping company, we weren't married. Afterward, there weren't a lot of possibilities. After a certain age and in certain jobs, you never meet anybody. There was supposed to be a new woman at the tax office in June, but she turned out to be a he—they hired a man.

For Brewster, the old woman he had sometimes spent time with, a sarcastic British lady named Mrs. Sims who also lived in the building, had died in the spring, so he was as alone as I was. After she died, he had broken into her apartment—the lock wasn't much—and taken a weird collection of stuff. He had photographs of her and him, a square jar full of sand, a slab of polished green and white malachite stone, and her hair dryer, a big old one with the bonnet in a round carrier, all on the shelves in his living room with books and magazines and a Civil War pistol that didn't shoot.

So I was up there playing cards one afternoon when there came this pounding on the door. The place shook. He got up and opened it and there stood Mrs. Eller, screaming, pointing down into the courtyard, a fenced space behind the building with a small swimming pool rimmed by stones set in concrete and stocked with white iron lawn furniture.

We were three floors up. We stepped out onto the walkway and looked down into the swimming pool where she was pointing. When we got downstairs we found the woman's orange striped cat in the pool. She said that old Abe and a couple of the others had chased it in there and drowned it, that it was terrified of the water. There was blood in the pool, too, a stain holding together, apparently from the head or ear. I got the skimmer and pushed it in under the cat and lifted him out, swung him over onto the stone. When I looked around Brewster stood behind me with his arms dull at his sides, his rugged hands quivering at the cuffs of his gray shirt. He was looking over my shoulder at the dead cat, inconsolable.

I have seen grown men cry, but Brewster was past seventy, and I had never seen an old man cry. It was a terrible thing. I put my arms around him. "C'mon," I said. "Let's go upstairs." I had this sick feeling in my stomach. I knew I should take care of Mrs. Eller, too, but I couldn't do both of them. I looked around, hoping one of the other old women would show up. Mrs. Eller was dull-eyed, opaque. "Sorry," I said.

It just got worse. A few days later, the Siamese, old Abe, disappeared, so I took off work and we spent all day and most of the night out looking. I was afraid of finding Abe dead on the road that ran in front of the apartments, though the cats didn't go out there much. A couple of days passed. Brewster was certain that Mrs. Eller had done it. He claimed that he had heard Abe calling—every Siamese has a distinctive voice, he said—from somewhere on the first floor. I laughed, and he looked at me. "It just seems... unlikely," I said. A week after that Brewster got a letter from the management company's lawyers which informed him that as he had violated the terms

81

of his lease by keeping animals on the premises and as those animals had become a nuisance to the other tenants, etc. etc. etc. They gave him two weeks.

Someone told him about an old house, across town, near a park, and I helped him pack, boxing and taping. He never would have gotten it done, didn't seem to care. There wasn't much to it. He lived a pretty spartan existence except for the cats and his wood work and what seemed to be every issue of *Prevention* magazine ever published. He had three drawers full of medicines, salves and pills and drops, not for him but for the cats. Brown prescription bottles with "Antibody Brewster" and "Abe" and "Moxy" and sometimes "cat" for the patient's name. He had a lot of clothes he never wore, books, some odds and ends. The apartment did smell, and packing it up seemed to make it worse. As we threw windows open to air it, I said, "I don't know why you care."

"They'll think they were right," he said. "They'll congratulate themselves."

All through the last few days of the packing I wanted to say something—some new and better way of phrasing "no"—but after that one time he never asked me again about moving in with him.

The day before he left he was still swearing that Mrs. Eller had stolen his cat. We had everything ready to go, in cartons by the door, and the manager had arranged a truck for his furniture. We played a half dozen games of whist, dealing cards out on top of the cardboard boxes, and then I got up to go home.

I looked around the bare living area. The remaining cats were all there in the front room, and it occurred to me that they were there because they were afraid of being left behind. "Hey, Brewster," I said, "I'm thinking about just staying here. I mean…" I shook my head, tried to get myself to look at him. "I'll think about it, but I'll probably just stay."

"Yeah, I figured," he said. He was standing up, waiting. It felt like he was pushing me out the door. "Listen, I want you to keep Killer. You know, the little one."

"I couldn't take her," I said.

"Oh sure you could."

"I'll see her over at your place," I said, and then a strange look flashed across his face for a second, and he abandoned the idea.

The next morning while the women were all gathered around the pool and the two guys the manager had hired were filling up a van with Brewster's furniture and boxes, he showed up at my door with a fat plastic garbage bag and this giant smile on his flawed, reddish old face. He laughed. "Here," he said, handing it to me. "Look what I found. And exactly where I said he'd be." I took the bag from him. It twitched; it was heavy. It was Abe, of course. Brewster had rescued him. That was the last time we saw each other.

•　•　•

But the daughter called again this morning. So here I am, like a fool. The house is canary yellow with a half-circle driveway in front under high pine trees. I park my car behind a rental Buick near the door and get out. I have bought and brought a plastic "cat carrier" but leave it on the passenger seat. When I push the doorbell, a short woman about forty years old in a black dress comes and opens the door. Her name is Susan. There'll be no funeral for Brewster; he's to be cremated. Only five cats are left—"The other one died a month ago," Susan says—and I wonder what she would've thought had she seen nine. The survivors are Killer, Abe, a small new gray tabby, and the twin black cats. So much for superstitions.

"There'll be almost twenty thousand dollars for you. Daddy was always pretty frugal, except for *them*," she says, looking affectionately at the cats, curled up together on a futon couch I don't recognize. "I'll hate to have to take them to the pound, but…" She shrugs.

The house looks inside much like Brewster's apartment always looked—comfortable, squared away—although that may be Susan's doing. There's a long counter, a serving bar between the kitchen and dining room, and arrayed on top are five or six of the fabric-covered boxes that Brewster made, along with a camera and his antique pistol. "You want that?" Susan asks when she notices me notice it. "Take anything you want, really."

"No, but thanks," I say.

There're lots of windows, lots of light. It's a nice old house. Open cartons on the floor show books, and the kitchen's completely done, with cabinet doors swung open, empty shelves, dishes and glasses and such swathed in newspapers in more cardboard cartons, waiting only to be sealed. Three big dark green "lawn and leaf" plastic bags are lined up beside the front door. Odd that I didn't see them before. His clothes, probably. They're the same sort of bag he had Abe inside five months ago. It occurs to me only now that the cat could've suffocated, for some reason a suddenly terrifying thought.

I look around, searching for Abe, to make sure I did see him, just now, and there he is, asleep, indifferent. I wonder if he is sad, if he knows that Brewster isn't ever coming back.

"So, which one is it?" Susan asks and slides to the couch

where the cats are, settles at one end and reaches out to pet the nearest.

"I'd like one of those boxes," I say, and when she gives me a puzzled look, "one of the cases he built, the camera case, or the one he made for the cassettes and CD's. They're beautiful things."

"Surely," she says, "anything you want. I'm shipping a few things north, but most of it is going to go to the trash or the Salvation Army, so don't be shy. It feels like throwing away his whole life."

I pick a box, a rectangular one the size of an encyclopedia, covered in gray material, and open it. The inside, finished in gray felt, is four long horizontal compartments, the last one divided into thirds. A fancy paper clip and two of those sleek blue pencils with black tips lie in one of the compartments. Staedtler. It's a beautiful thing. What was this for? The box closes perfectly, and then holds closed with no need to flip the tiny brass latch. And it comes into my mind: Brewster's been completely alone for five months.

"Now I wish I had come down here more than a couple times," she says. "I feel so selfish." She looks teary, then slips into her thoughts, a vacant look, and shakes her head slowly side to side.

"Susan, I don't mean to be weird, but I don't want the money," I say. "Do something with it for me, will you?"

"Don't think I can do that," she says. "Legally, I mean."

"I'll write a letter. Give it to the Humane Society or something. I'm serious. I absolutely can't take it." I hold my hands up, palms out. "It's wrong," I say, as if that made any sense, and walk up to the couch. The snowshoe cat seems to recognize me, steps across the futon and offers its cheek for my hand.

"This'd be the one," I say. "He called it 'Killer.'" Involuntarily I laugh and Susan looks at me and laughs, too. I raise my free hand to my face and try to force a straight expression, but laugh again.

"Well, I'm sure you'll take good care of her," she says. "There's some more stuff in that front bedroom—" She points. "—if you want to look at it. I'd rather you had it than nobody." She stands up and smoothes her skirt, lifts her purse from a table, back to being business like. She's leaving. "I've got to go back by the funeral home that's handling things, and the supermarket. More tape, more boxes. I'm sorry, I don't mean to be rude. But you'll be all right. And seriously, it wouldn't bother me if the whole place was empty when I got back. Just pull the door to when you leave. There're two big bags of that special veterinary cat food in the laundry room. It'll just go to waste otherwise." She points past the kitchen. "It was nice to meet you. Daddy really loved you, I think." She walks on out, shuts the door behind her, and there's the sound of a car door and the engine firing, then complete silence.

It feels weird being there by myself so I collect the gray box in one hand and Killer in the other hand and walk out and put them in my car, then come back inside for the bags of cat food. The other cats follow to the door as I carry away the two heavy bags. I put the bags in the trunk, then get in the car and sit for a while looking at his house. It's quiet. I can't leave, it's as if something's holding me there, I'm starting to get really spooky. I wish to God she hadn't left first. I wish she'd come back. I wish, I wish, I wish.

• • •

The cats go limp, legs hanging free, when I carry them out to the car, one after another, one in each hand, as if they've known all along that they're going with me and have been waiting only for the idea to show up in my mind. The car's full of their faces.

I'm projecting, no doubt. They're just cats, stepping around on the upholstery, sniffing things, sidling between the seats, settling, jumping, finding spots, all eyes. I feel better now though, and glance back up at the house, at the yellow door. "*Okay?*" I ask, and reach out to turn the key, and as the engine starts, the car rocks a little.

Sale

Quinn sold the car one Friday morning in the parking lot of his new apartment complex. The buyer trembled as the two of them walked around the car. A skinny, very fair man in a pink oxford shirt, deathly pale in the morning sunlight. When he reached out and ran his finger along a deep crease in the front fender, Quinn nodded. "That dent tells a story," he said, and laughed. The guy crouched and stared hard down the length of the car, looking for waves in the body panels. Something he read in a magazine article, Quinn thought. He can't see a thing. Jesus, somebody should tell him not to wear pink shirts. Looks like the inside of a watermelon. Name is probably Allen or something. The man stood by the driver's door, staring inside.

"My wife's car," Quinn said. "Ex-wife. Her ex-car. She... she—We're divorced. She spent too much time with the neighbor down the street."

"Looks in good shape," the pale guy said.

Quinn nodded. "He was on television, a weatherman; on weekends. She thought he was some kind of star." Jesus, he thought. His face. Watermelon rind.

"Can we start it up?" the guy said.

"What? Sure, here." Quinn handed him the keys. "Need to goose it a couple times, get some gas on the way."

The guy started the car. "You mind if I have a friend of

mine look it over?" He sat in the driver's seat with one leg hanging out the open door and leaned forward, listening to the engine. "That ticking normal?"

Quinn shrugged. "I know from ticking, right? How about nine hundred? Two bills for ticking. You know that dent I showed you?" Quinn said. "They were parked in front of the house, one night. I was inside, watching *Masterpiece Theater*, and I heard brakes and then this shriek, like somebody pulling a rack out of a gigantic oven. I ran outside and there was my wife and the weatherman, and some kid with one of those stupid trucks, the ones way up in the air with the airplane tires?

"My wife was buttoning her shirt. The weatherman, he's giving the kid a hundred bucks, a hundred dollar bill. He's doing my wife right on the street in front of my house, and he carries around hundred dollar bills." Quinn looked around the perfect, empty parking lot. "So I moved here." The apartments were red brick, almost orange. A low chain-link fence ran along the edge of the parking lot.

"I'm sorry," the guy said.

"She didn't want to be ordinary, I guess. And he was on TV." Quinn drew himself full height and threw his arm out, drawing in the air with a finger. "You know, pointing to those swirly lines with the pimples." He screwed up his face in a lurid smile. "It's a cold front, here... so get out the fuzzy wuzzies tonight—" His hand hung in the air, pointing to an imaginary map. "Stars," he said, and shook his head. "I still watch him, every weekend."

The pale guy looked at the car.

"Why don't you just take it?" Quinn said. "Just get it out of here." The car was a big green Chrysler, nine years old. It looked stupid in the parking lot, in the evenings, when all the Hondas and Toyotas and the GM copies of them and a few

Jaguars and Corvettes and one black Porsche came home. "Just take it. Have you got ten bucks?"

"I'm really sorry."

Quinn laughed. "Hey, don't be. That's life, right? Thing that bothers me is, I wanted to call the cops. I mean that's what I thought: Call the cops; get the kid a ticket; square it with the insurance. But he was right. Give the kid a hundred dollars. Burns me up. That's what we have stars for. They always know what to do." He smiled.

In a green car, Quinn thought, he looks even stranger. Extraordinary. People'll say, Allen, where'd you get that car? Hey everybody! Look at Allen's new car.

Vexed

There was never a chance I'd be anything but his brother or she would be anything but his girlfriend, but I had gotten mixed up with my brother's ex-girlfriend anyway. It was obviously a stupid idea, but things are obvious to you only if you don't mind them being so. And, anyway, many and rich pleasures attach to stupid behavior.

It was about four a.m. and twenty degrees when my rock—a little heavier than I thought—broke right on through Teresa's window, dropping into her apartment. *No*, I thought, and glass splashed down the side of the apartment building and onto the sidewalk at my feet.

Before I could move, Allen, my big little brother, was standing at the window looking down at me. I owed him money, which was one reason that he wasn't already downstairs beating me to a pulp. Teresa is his sometime girlfriend—they're trying to "patch it up" he tells me. What she tells me is that she's finished with him, that it's "done, over" and I believe her until Allen comes to her window at four in the morning. Allen is twenty-six and I'm twenty-nine, and I borrow money from him and take Teresa out to dinner. I should've told Allen that I'd been seeing Teresa, but he can get ugly.

"What do you want, Webster?" he said, thinking I came to see him. That he couldn't imagine it otherwise was insulting, in a way. "Are you vexed, or something?"

Once I read a Russian novel, a translation, and then I went around saying "vexed" all the time. In the novel, a great many people were "vexed." It was maybe ten years ago, but Allen has never let me forget it. It has always been his way of reminding me that I was nerdish, that he was taller, stronger, tougher than I was. He missed that moment late in high school when it became clear that that no longer mattered. His ex-girlfriend's affection for me would not compute in Allen's conception of the world. Bye bye Mr. Soloflex. Hello, Vexed.

He had slid the broken window up and was standing there, fully dressed, and staring at me like I was from some other galaxy. From his expression I guessed it was him who was vexed, likely having one of those pained "talks" that two people have at four in the morning fully dressed, those tight, strained conversations in which she is telling you she doesn't care for you but you refuse to hear it, and if it's at the beginning of your time with her you're right to refuse to hear because she might just be giving herself room to operate, but if it's at the end of your time with her, you are wrong, and she wants only for you to go away.

This was what was going through my mind, along with a desire to kill him, as I stood on the sidewalk freezing. This was what I wanted Teresa to be saying. Teresa is five foot eleven, and she runs, in shiny spandex and a T-shirt. Teresa has sleepy green eyes and a cat's smile. She sings. Walks around the apartment singing, *My momma done told me / When I was a baby...* But you don't love a woman because her voice is beautiful and her foolish belief that she is ten pounds overweight is an illusion, and she's so lovely it makes you weep. Teresa thinks she just might possibly love me, and that's what makes you love a woman, that possibility. If she's sure she loves you, if it's a certainty, you get overconfident, even indifferent, but if it's only a possibility, you are finished. Maybe it's different for other people, I don't know.

"Stay right there," Allen said, finally, leaning out and looking down at me. "I want to talk to you." I felt sick. The cold was coming through my jacket like it was paper.

Two months before when Teresa threw Allen out, he didn't much concern himself about it, but when he found out that she was seeing someone, he was suddenly all over her again. Lilies, no less. Earrings. When I suggested he probably had found the earrings, on his carpet, Teresa got mad at me. It took all I had not to tell Teresa that that was, in fact, exactly where he had gotten them. He told me. This whole thing is not bringing out the best in any of us.

While Allen was on his way downstairs, Teresa came to the window for a second and looked at me. Just looked. She was wearing jeans and an oxford shirt, white, maybe pale yellow, near as I could tell. She looked sad, worn out.

"I'll fix it, next week," I said. "The window. I'm sorry." She gave me that sleepy-eyed smile and turned away from the window. I had thought she would find it romantic, pebbles on the glass, standing shivering down below her bower and so on, but it hadn't occurred to me that the glass was cheap and cold and the rock had to be sized accordingly. And I threw a little too hard maybe, afraid of missing the window entirely.

"I'm glad to see you," Allen said. I took a step back toward my car as he walked up, stocky, zipping his leather jacket and breathing a little heavy. His eyes were very beautiful, blue. My eyes, my dead father's eyes. "Let's go over to my place," he said. "Get out of this weather."

I followed him to his apartment, a big place on the fifteenth floor of a fifteen story high rise building with an underground garage. I parked on the street, and by the time I got upstairs, he had made himself tea and was sitting at his kitchen table watching the television in the living room, with the sound muted. Tea, I thought. Since when does Allen drink tea?

"Well, Webster, what are we going to do?" he said. "Want a cup?" He lifted his, pointed to a saucepan of steaming water on the stove in the kitchen. The apartment was big and very white, walls, rugs, even the table he was sitting at was hot white formica. Frost on the windows. A pillow and sheets and blankets were lying on the living room rug, as if he'd been sleeping there. The rest of the place somehow looked a little in disarray, too. "Tea?" he said.

I shook my head. "You got a beer?"

"Help yourself," he said. "Course it's probably not that fancy German stuff you like."

"Anything with bubbles is fine," I said, taking a bottle from the bright white refrigerator.

"So what are we going to do about this?" he said, and pushed out a chair for me with his foot. "About you hounding my girlfriend."

I was looking at his bull neck, the big tendons or whatever they are standing out at the side, looking like rope. "She told you."

"She told me nothing, bighead. Boy, you really do think I'm stupid, don't you?" He took a long, slow breath and then sighed. "Just because you're so goddamn smart doesn't mean I'm stupid."

He was right, I knew. A bad habit, underestimating other people, a habit I hate in my friends, probably because I do it myself.

He sipped his tea. "This is hurting me, you know? This..." He didn't finish. He looked around the L-shaped living-dining room, stared for an instant at one of the lamps on which the shade was crooked, then looked into his cup. "She's the best woman I ever had, best one I'll ever have a chance of, and now big brother is sneaking around, reciting poetry and junk. Taking her to little boutiquey restaurants, on money he borrowed from me."

"Money's real important to you, isn't it, Allen?"

"It's important to you when the waiter brings the check, isn't it? Don't Gandhi me, Web, okay? I haven't been doing real well, lately. You don't make much of a Gandhi, anyway. I mean, you're kind of soft, easy, self-indulgent, and libertine."

"Me?" I said. "I'll be going now, little brother." I got up to leave, set the beer down. "You were fooling around on Teresa from day one. Yes sir, you're a regular ascetic—blondes and brunettes only. She threw you out, remember? And you're calling me a libertine? You know what the word means?" A mistake.

But he just shrugged. "Okay, so you're just soft and self-indulgent," he said. "The difference is, I don't pretend to be Gandhi." He waved his hand and sighed again. "How much of your interest in Teresa is because she's my girlfriend? You ever think about that?"

"Yeah. She isn't anymore. Your girlfriend. Yeah, I thought about it." I sat back down across the table from him, circled the beer bottle with my fingers. He was watching me, sipping the tea, waiting. There was some look on his face. Certainty, confidence.

"I couldn't figure it." I looked at him. "I don't know," I said. He was smirking. But maybe he wasn't. "Anymore. Anything. I don't know." It was as if he wasn't even interested in our conversation anymore. His face was the big, quiet face of a child, of Allen as a child, of a time when it seemed that everyone knew what was going on but me. He had always been this way. And I thought, It never ends.

I stood up from his table, tried to say goodbye but couldn't, waved and then walked out and down the hall to the elevator, still there from when I'd come up in it. I remembered being in the hospital room with my father two weeks before he died, and I said something to him about coughing, only the way I said it it sounded like *coffin*, and my father looked at me, startled, with a look of terror on his face. And I thought about my own dying, and suddenly it was obvious that Teresa didn't, couldn't and wouldn't ever care for me. I hadn't the confidence for it. The elevator doors drew open, and I got on.

Pretend She Don't Scare You a Bit

My giant yellow stepladder shifted, then rose up on one foot, and a minute later I was there, on the concrete, like that, sweetly, aimlessly recalling the history of my escape. Now I'm in the hospital. Can I move my arms and legs? Yes, I can, now I can. It was yesterday I was sort of paralyzed.

I'm working in school supplies, next to pet supplies. Charlene brushes past me, lets her hand drag across my butt, laughs. "So close, but yet..." I say. Her smock is untied and her blue silk blouse is unbuttoned halfway down. "Dream on, college," she says. She takes a box of pencils and slips it into her blouse, then draws the smock tight and ties it. Charlene steals things, for fun mostly. I do, too. There isn't a lot of fun working in a place like this.

I go back to work, watching the white metal ceiling for the bird that sails around in the steelwork and surveillance cameras up there. A starling. It got in months ago, but it hasn't been around for at least a week, so maybe they were right, and it died of thirst like they said it would.

Charlene's boyfriend, Patricio, dumped her last week for a black girl on dayshift named Lakeshia. Patricio is my best friend here. He's big. Charlene is small, short, sexy, in a Spanish sort of way. The stuff that dreams are made of.

In the pet shop there's a kid looking into a fish tank, hands around his face, forehead on the glass, staring into the aquarium. Guy's about twelve. The store is Wannabe Wal-Mart, it's near midnight on a Friday, we never close. I'm sale-ing stuff, putting on Manager's Special stickers, $1.99, a hundred and twenty boxes of pencils. It's a trick. The computers'll pick the new price up anyway, and there's a sign on the shelf, but they think the customers like to see these stickers.

I wish I could be there staring in at the neon tetras, watching them zoom around. At least they enjoy their little pointless lives. We used to have a baby boa constrictor, but it died. It was really murder, the dumbass store management murdered it. They wanted $99.00 for it. Duh. Like they've never seen who shops here.

"When you going to take me out to dinner?" Charlene says, bumps me a little with her hip. "I am off at two."

"I can't afford you. I eat peanut butter and jelly."

"Oh, I *love* peanut butter and jelly," she says, and licks her lips. "White bread."

"Well, okay, good. I'll pick you up, ten after two. Hey, Charlene, what do you do with all the stuff you swipe?"

"I don't know what you talking about, college boy," she says. "You need a rain gauge? A Beretta? Some car wax? You go to law school, you can defen' me, okay? I pay you in merchandise." She flips her shining, shoulder-length hair, and from nowhere produces the box of pencils and tosses it back on my shelf. "I got pencils," she says. "Two o'clock."

I watch her walk away, swaying. She's a certain kind of sexy, buys expensive clothes, wears them a little loose, walks good, the voice, knows how to look at you, smiles. A woman who knows everything. You look at her and think, Nothing I could ever do would make this woman nervous. And then she's out of sight. I look up into the white steel rafters.

Later, after I'm off, in the back Patricio comes up to me carrying a pool cue in each hand. "Man, you poaching my woman?" he says, and stares hard, until he starts laughing and I breathe out. "First thing she did was come to tell me, cholo," he says. "Here, you're gonna need some of these. Rocket fuel." He puts a couple pills in my shirt pocket.

"She wasn't serious," I say.

"Serious?" Patricio says. "She is desperate. Just pretend she don't scare you a bit." He holds one of the cue sticks out to me. "Take this. We gonna get that bird. He been back here all night. Been shitting all over the stock."

Outside the breakroom is the warehouse area, the stock piled on pallets in rows, like a lumberyard or a library. Patricio's got big yellow fourteen foot ladders at opposite ends of the long, narrow space.

"There he is," Patricio says, pointing up to the starling sitting on the bottom of one of the exposed steel joists. "Bird-ball," he says, grinning, and swings his pool cue like a bat. "I be Sammy Sosa, you be that red guy." He means Mark McGwire.

We climb the ladders and run the pool cues along the corrugated steel of the roof for the racket it makes, to start the bird flying. Air must be twenty degrees warmer up here. As soon as the starling lights somewhere we shout and bash at the ceiling again, and he's off again. The ladders rock and shudder as we slash at him and he flutters out of range until one time Patricio swings and almost falls, and the starling jumps franti-cally straight up and thumps against the ceiling, then drops four feet and swoops back toward me on the far side of the ladder, in perfect position, rising, floating, right in the center of the strike zone. It feels like I'm shaking my head but I'm not moving. I'm leaning.

My arms jerk the pool cue out horizontal, for a bunt. He

doesn't hit it. He stops on it, instantly, bobs over head first and rights himself, then spins around, weird, dance-y footwork, to face the other way. He's black, green, feathers iridescent as his wings disappear, gasping for breath, watching me with one coral-colored eye. He is perfection. "You got him!" Patricio yells. I have got him, I think. And of course right there the ladder starts to move.

Good Parts

I

Bill was staring at his eyes in the bathroom mirror. Blue eyes. Some gray in them. "It's your sense of inadequacy," Bill said.

"What's my sense of inadequacy?" Maureen said. Dark hair. Green eyes.

"Why you always fail. Why you can't do anything right. Me too."

"You too what?"

"I have the same problem. We share this problem."

Maureen stood up, walked out. She looked like a model. Took her robe, cigarettes, beer.

"Bitch," Bill said, staring into the mirror. "Stupid bitch."

Maureen fell asleep in the living room, on the couch. Again, Bill thought. I was a jerk again. I must have been born a jerk. He rearranged the robe, to cover her.

II

Bill and Maureen stopped at the laundromat and left their clothes, went to the grocery store, stopped off at the library, went to the drugstore, picked up their laundry.

Maureen made stroganoff from a package that advertised itself as taking eight minutes. Bill sliced up the steak. Checked her progress. "Those sure are funny looking noodles," Bill said. "They're crooked."

"These fine noodles..." Maureen said. "You're gonna *love* these noodles."

Bill read *Newsweek* until dinner was ready. Twenty minutes. They had candlelight and wine.

"I love these noodles," Bill said.

III

Maureen left the house crying. Slammed the car door. She drove to her friend Jane's house. Jane's house smelled like soup. There was a cloth tea strainer on the counter, very brown.

"He wants to sleep around and you can't," Jane said. "What does he think, you don't want to? The Neanderthal. Want some tea?" Jane got up. "Here, read this magazine. And this one. And this one."

"Stay out of it," Maureen said.

IV

Bill took the mop from Maureen. "Not like that," he said. "Like *this*." He was showing her how to use a sponge-mop. He held the mop in his hands, a yellow handle, a yellow sponge.

"Like *that*?"

"You have to drag it so it's flat on the floor, then you get

the whole surface, not just the front edge. The bottom surface."
He pulled the mop expertly across the linoleum, holding the
handle at an awkward forward angle of 80 degrees.

Maureen ran into the closet and began screaming with
laughter.

Bill opened the closet door and looked at the tears in her
wet eyes, the shirt wadded in her fist. "Foolish?" he said.

V

Bill and Maureen sat on the carpet in the living room playing
Black Tower until 6 a.m.

VI

At the office a handsome young millionaire talked to Maureen. A client. He looked out the window as he talked, at parking lots fifteen stories below. Maureen typed, printed forms.
Her boss was "in conference." She missed lunch.

The young millionaire described in lavish detail his va-
cation which had been spent in Mexico, Puerto Vallarta and
Cozumel. He talked about "little bars." He intimated that he
had had sex with beautiful women.

Maureen told Bill about the young millionaire when she
got home. "He's a jerk," Maureen said.

Bill laughed.

"But he's a millionaire."

Maureen swirled an imaginary Tequila Sunrise and did

her young millionaire imitation, lifted her eyebrows and spoke through her nose:

"Oh yes, I own several tall buildings. I have eaten turtle eggs inside the turtle. Ahem. The inside of the turtle is hot and pink. My love life? Ha! It's understandable you would be curious. I am a man of the world who has made love to an eyeguana, pretty thing. Of course you wouldn't know… It wasn't just any iguana—it was a bisexual iguana. After, we shared a cigarette. He said I was the best he'd ever had."

VII

Bill went to the bookstore. Once a week. He had his eye on a girl there, a slow thin girl who worked in the bookstore.

"Can I help you," the girl said.

"Yes, please take me home," Bill said.

"Sure," the girl said.

"What?"

"I get off in an hour."

I have been following women around bookstores for twelve years, Bill thought, in the car. The girl came out and got into the car, and they drove to her apartment which was full of hateful, expensive furniture and liquor bottles facing front. Bill had four drinks and made love to her.

"Stay the night," the girl said.

Bill thought about it for an hour and then said, "I can't. I want to, but I can't." Everything about the apartment was wrong; the toothpaste was on the wrong side of the bathroom sink.

VIII

Bill bought a gun, .38 caliber. It smelled good. Maureen returned it and got his money back. $199.95.

IX

The dentist told Maureen she needed some work. An assistant took it all down. At the reception counter Maureen wrote out a check and asked for a chart of the proposed work and charges.

The woman behind the counter looked up at her. "May I ask what you want it for?" she said.

"What?"

"May I ask why you need it?"

Maureen dropped her cigarette onto the carpet, grinding at it with her shoe. "Sure, honey, it's because it's my teeth and my money."

In the lobby of the building she called Bill from a pay phone. He was at work. She was crying.

"They want nineteen hundred dollars. They want to butcher my teeth. They want to fix—my teeth don't hurt. Why do—I've got three month's worth of appointments," Maureen said.

"I'll pick you up," Bill said.

"I've got my car."

"I'll pick you up anyway. Call them back and cancel the appointments. We'll try another dentist. Second opinion, like that. Fifteen minutes."

X

Maureen made a meatloaf and a salad.

"Thanks for dinner," Bill said, after they had finished.

"Is she pretty? How old is she? Did you tell her about us? Is she good at it? Screwing? Better than me? Is she blonde? What's her name? Don't tell me. Is she more beautiful than me? I don't want to know anything about it," Maureen said.

Bill felt sick to his stomach.

"Did you have a good time?"

XI

Maureen went to a bar with one of the law clerks from the office. He was short. Maureen was older and taller. When he began telling her about his "mistress" she excused herself and went home.

"This is not working," she said, at the kitchen table. "We're going to have to try something else."

"One little slip?" Bill said.

"That's not it," Maureen said. "It's more than that. I'm moving."

"I think you're right," Bill said. "I think we should get two apartments, like we talked about."

"I mean moving out of town. I'm leaving town. I'm going back to school."

"Wait. Now wait—"

"No waiting. I thought today maybe six years from now I could meet you on a street in Mexico, you know, outside a 'little bar' or something, and then we'd have a lot to talk about, we could go to the beach and screw and talk all night long."

"It's movies," Bill said. "It won't happen."

"It could happen," she said. "That's the point."

Bill shook his head.

"It won't happen *this* way, that's for sure," she said.

"It's crap," he said.

"There'll be iguanas. And those funny birds, yakking."

"Maureen—"

"You won't even bitch about the sand," she said. "The waves will make those wave noises. There'll be wind. There'll be colored lights. You'll be crazy and happy again. There'll be cliffs. Cliffs behind us. Cliffs." Dark hair. Green eyes.

In the Rain

She was a nice wife, even liked me for a time. I enjoyed her company, and in the early days, when sleeping together had this scorched-earth sort of magic, we mistook that for love. But the magazine articles she sometimes gave me didn't make sense to me. I could never find a description of what it's like. One summer a twenty-two year old girl came to work at the bank as a teller—I was training them then—and she was pretty and young and below her wide, flat forehead her gaudy green eyes had a hint of confusion or even hurt in them. I was seduced; she was interested. I waited for her to arrive at work in the morning and maneuvered to be by the elevator or in the corridor, for two minutes of her. We went to lunch a few times, talked at some dreary bank parties. Unable to touch her, I stood against a white wall in some excessively carpeted middle management home, talking to her, staring, trembling. I want. That is what it is like. Insufficiently tidy. It's unkind to ask a man to have feelings. This is what I was thinking, standing in the rain, the day the cat came back. But that was later.

At work people say I'm "distant," my family was sort of cool and rational—I mean they weren't always playing kissy face with one another—and last winter when my wife left, she said living with me was like living in dry ice. "You've no feelings," she said, and I told her that that wasn't logical, that it was only reasonable to assume that, in regard to feelings, everyone had an exactly equal amount. She said, "See what I mean." One of those things women say when they're angry.

When she left me the cat, asked me to keep it for her, she said, "Maybe old Rilkey will teach you something." I thought maybe she had a boyfriend, one who didn't like cats, not that I blame him. Talk about cold. They really do look for someone who can't stand them, and then just jump up on his lap. This cat wasn't so bad. I'd always hated its name, though, so I started calling him "Slick." It took him three or four months to learn it, not because he was stupid, just because he was obstinate. Last week in the floods, his obstinacy almost got him killed.

It rained for six days. Lawns were like sponges, the air in the house was thick and wet, streets were impassable and everywhere there was mud. By the time the cat dragged himself in on the fifth day, I'd given him up for drowned. He was soaked, black fur lying flat in little gobs all over his body so that it didn't look like fur anymore. I loved him. That's a feeling, isn't it?

It was a Monday, June 9, when it started raining. I let Slick out in the morning when I left for work. My wife used to put him out at night but I never do unless he makes himself such a pain I can't stand it. Anyway I let him out and left for the bank. I'm a loan officer. You get callous after years of listening to people's troubles, especially when you can't always do what they want. They lie to you, anyway. Hell, if it was my money, I'd just give it to them, like I did when I was a teller. It's only paper. That's how everybody who works in a bank thinks, and why sometimes you just take some of it home. Sometimes you give it to other people.

About three that afternoon, Becky, my assistant, told me there was a storm coming in and a few minutes later, as if on cue, the world got dark. Out my windows, low black clouds. I left early.

When I got back to the house, Slick wasn't around, but

I didn't notice until around eleven-thirty that night when I went into the kitchen and mixed my nightcap—a tall Scotch and water. I carried the glass over and opened the back door and whistled. By then it'd been raining seven hours straight, so I figured he'd be in the garage, contrite for staying out so late. I whistled again, stood by the door. Took a sip of the drink. Suit yourself, I thought. I stood a minute and listened to the thunderstorm.

That was one thing we used to do together sometimes, my wife and I, if there was a storm, we'd have a drink and leave the door open, cut the lights, watch the lightning and listen to the rain. And smoke, before we quit smoking.

The next morning, Tuesday, it was still raining and the cat still wasn't back when I left for work. I drove to the office under the gloomy, gray skies listening to the rain beating on the windshield and the ripping sound the car tires made on the wet streets, thinking. I have crooked little feelings, I guess, nothing you could write a magazine article about. Not like these people with these giant, rectangular emotions that sound like volumes of an encyclopedia. Guilt, Hysteria, Independence, Joy, Loss, Zed. Rot.

Sometime that morning I told Becky that my cat was out in the rain overnight. "Slick?" she said—I didn't even know she knew his name. "You didn't go out and find him?" It was strange to me that she would get so excited. I said, "Becky, it was pouring. I wouldn't know where to find him, anyway. I don't know where he goes." The look on her exquisitely made up face, framed in blonde-edged brown curls, was dismissive, damning.

"I whistled for him," I said, raising my voice. All along the hall there, the clerical people were looking at me, so I tried to speak normally. "I was out calling him and calling him, for an hour." But she knew I was lying, she'd turned back to the computer by then.

The weather was making everybody edgy. I did like the cat, a great deal. It was just the way I understood things—cats went out and later they came back. They're animals. You don't ask them where they've been and what they've been doing. Next thing you know the cat'll be telling me I've got to learn to "let go" and "share my feelings" and "cuddle." Jesus.

At home that evening I went out and called for the cat from both the kitchen door, that opens into the garage, and from the back bedroom windows, at the opposite end of the house. Then I remembered that once when we had first had the cat, when he was just a few months old, a kitten, pint-size, he was gone overnight and my wife and I had found him the next day, up on the roof of the house, whining. I found him, actually, and my wife gushed on and on about it, and I felt like a hero.

So I pulled on my raincoat, and got out the big red umbrella, and I got outside in the rain and walked back and forth around the house looking up on the roof. Of course Slick wasn't up there. Dumb, I thought. The cat's not on top of something, he's under something somewhere. I went out and called him again around midnight, but he didn't show, so I had an extra Scotch and went to sleep.

By Wednesday morning it had been raining solid for two days and the TV morning show and my soggy newspaper were talking about how many inches of rain it was and how the ground was saturated and the two rivers were cresting north of town. Water was driving snakes and deer into people's yards and so on. My house smelled damp, muggy; you couldn't get away from it. In the neighborhood, water was standing every-where, and the little creek had turned into an ugly torrent. The underpass on the street that I usually took to work was full of water. You could just see the tip of the black and white stick, the flood gauge, and the stick was six feet. I had to drive about ten blocks up, past the park, to get across under the Loop.

All the way into work I dreaded Becky asking me if I had found the cat, and that was the first thing she said. When I told her I hadn't, she frowned and went back to her keyboard. Outside the windows, gray sheets of water coming down. We didn't talk again all day, until close to five when she was packing up to leave.

"You know, sometimes they get up under the house," she said. "Is there a space under your house?"

I said there was, but it was probably a bog by now. I told her I would look there, with a flashlight.

Even when it's dry, you have to get down on your belly to look under the house, but I had promised Becky. When I got home and the cat was still not back, I changed into some jeans and a sweatshirt and put my raincoat on over that and went out in the rain with a flashlight to the place in the back garden where there's an opening in the outside wall down to the space under the house. The garden was full of water.

I slid through the mud and into the opening, my face about ten inches into the two foot high space under the house. You could see fifteen or twenty feet to either side. Rusty pipes hung under the floor and pools of oily water filled in the low spots and cobwebs glistened with drops of condensation in the flashlight beam. There was a thirty-year-old Coke bottle and a big pipe elbow with a crack in it. A rotting magazine. Spiders. A rat, fur flat and soaking wet. Dead. I pulled back out from under there.

My clothes were drenched by this time, and the whole front of me was so filthy I felt like a kid. I rolled over in the water in the garden to get mud all over the back of me too. I was laughing, taking a mud bath. I sat up against the back wall of the house and shielded my eyes with my hand to look at my neighbor's house. He has a better life than I have, I thought, and he's a Republican. It's not supposed to be that way. He even loves that fetishistic little dog. Think I'll just sit here until my cat comes home. I tried to pick up some mud, but it drained through my fingers, so I dug down and got drier dirt, and brought it up and compressed it into a clod, and threw it at his house. Clods for clods, I thought. Cat's dead. Life is stupid, most of it.

On Thursday it was still raining, and I didn't go to work. I started in, drove down the service road along the Loop until, near the cross street I'd found to get under the freeway, I saw a dead cat, an orange tabby, lying out from the curb, splitting the water running in the gutter. The service road was wide and ran beside a flat, empty park. Not far away, the same creek from near my house ran parallel along the other border of the park.

I jerked the car over, stopped, and got out. The cat's thick orange and white fur lay almost flat, like carpet. A big cat, stiff, not as big as Slick. It was pretty far from home. As I stood there in the rain, the weirdest thing happened—I almost started to cry. Now, my wife was right, actually, about my not having feelings, because I just don't. I remember one time she read me a magazine article about how the average man is five foot ten and cries once a month. I thought, Once a month? You've got to be kidding.

I couldn't go to work, so I picked the orange cat up and set it on the grass, so no one would hit it, then got back into my car and drove home, wishing I had a cigarette the way you wish for a cigarette after a few years of not smoking, wistful, wanting to be some way you used to be.

At home, I got my umbrella and then walked up and down the streets, methodically, block by block, looking, staring up driveways and into backyards, shouting Slick's name. I'd ask kids I saw if they'd seen a big black cat. I was wearing the raincoat and holding the red umbrella and walking through water that was often over my cuffs and sometimes up to my knees. The rain slanted in under the umbrella, but once you get good and soaked it doesn't much matter. Odd, really, the way we try to avoid the rain, stay dry, as if it hurt.

I walked up and down, opened people's gates, jumped fences, crossed patios. Sometimes people's cats would watch me from a windowsill and I'd knock at the house and ask about mine. I would finish one street and then start the next, block after block. Slogging through the water I got hunches and premonitions—he's in this block, or, Buicks, he likes Buicks. I saw black spots which turned out to be buckets, holes, hunks of mud, tree stumps, a black T-shirt wadded into a ball.

After four days of rain there was garbage everywhere—cups, a golf club, three or four shoes, a dog's collar, panties, a can of green beans. I was out all morning and into the afternoon, getting crazier, starting to get hot flashes and sweating in the rain, and starting to love the cat, desperately, wanting him back.

I finally got to the creek which was now angry, fifteen feet across, loud, shushing ahead like a picture in fast forward. I stopped, watching tree branches race past, then started to walk along beside it. If he got caught in this, I thought, he's gone. He was so clumsy he could barely make it across the living room rug without stumbling. So careless he'd fall asleep under a rocking chair. So insecure he wouldn't eat unless you stood there and watched. You could barely tell the fool was a cat.

As I walked along the creek bank, staying back from the

edge, slipping and sliding, I kept thinking he couldn't have wandered this far, but then I thought: It explains why he hasn't come home—he crossed it before the rain and then couldn't get back. Or, he tried to get back.

Eventually when I looked up, I was in the park. It was about three in the afternoon. I was on the opposite side of the park from the service road, but a concrete footbridge led over the fat angry creek, so I crossed and went to look for the orange tabby.

It was still lying where I'd left it that morning, but its mouth seemed to have opened slightly, baring the small front teeth. It was ugly. I knelt down to pick it up, and looked around. No one was ever going to find it here.

Carrying the cat under my raincoat I walked across the park, back across the bridge, and then along the creek, all the way to my neighborhood, and back up to my house. I set the cat on the front lawn, and stood looking down in the rain, thinking of it as a sort of signal, a crooked totem. A message to my cat, about what could happen. It lay out there the rest of the afternoon, all night, and most of the next morning.

I found Slick lying sprawled on the garage concrete, shivering, clumsy, careless. Obstinate. I carried him in and set him on the kitchen floor. On the white linoleum, limp, he looked like an embryo, his breaths heaving in the thin blue skin over his flanks, too tired to protest as I wrapped him in a towel and went over him with a hair dryer, blubbering like a baby. Later, I took a shovel from the garage and went to bury the other one. Standing out in the rain thinking, *This doesn't mean anything.* It just kept on raining.

Acquaintance

On the plane the gin happy flight attendants had had a hard time persuading anyone to sing Auld Lang Syne, but then finally, when they offered a free flight as well as the bottle of champagne, a little bald guy in a red coat got up, took the microphone, stood in the aisle posing like a 50's crooner, steadying himself with one hand on the back of a seat. The little guy had a very beautiful voice, and by the time he was finishing up the whole plane was singing, just as the seatbelt lights went on for the descent into Logan.

A nice thing, Quinn thought. He was sitting on the bed in his hotel room, on the phone with his father.

"You remember, Dad," Quinn said. "McCarthey was one of my teachers. I'm picking up some stuff I left in a rent house here. His book, other stuff. It's a fool's errand. Listen, I've got to go."

"Four hundred dollar flight, isn't it?" his father said. "Must be some book. You could still stop through here."

"I can't, Dad. I'd like to, but I'm back at work Tuesday. I just wanted to say Happy New Year. I'll call when I get back to Chicago, okay? I love you." He said goodbye and hung up. Tomorrow, Quinn thought. Get it and then get out of here. He settled back on the pale yellow brocade bedspread in the too bright hotel room, and closed his eyes. Four hundred dollar book, no less. Daddy's voice, he thought.

Quinn had not known, when he had been a student, that

T. Tyrone McCarthey was famous enough to get even the tiny news item about his death that the newspaper had run in the book section, six lines that called him a "modernist" and his career "disappointing" and even mentioned *White Cats*, the book he had signed, the same book Quinn had left in a cardboard box of books and other junk in an attic in a rent house in Brookline eight years ago when he finally finished school and left Boston for good.

McCarthey had been a fat, balding, red-faced man— around school they always said he was on speed, which may have been why he died at fifty-four. Quinn had been a sort of protege, for about a year, and then, about the time Quinn switched over to marketing, there was an argument. One night, drunk in a bar on Comm Ave., McCarthey thought Quinn had insulted Anna, his wife, and blew up, leaning into the younger man's face, screaming, his own huge red forehead swelling, shining, reflecting the red and blue neon of beer signs. Quinn just stood in the narrow corridor between the barstools and the tables, looking into McCarthey's face, dumb, trying not to cry, every muscle in his body tight, thinking how loud the voice was and how suddenly quiet the bar was, watching. Even now his jaw clenched. The wait, until the tirade was finally over, until McCarthey turned away, threw a bill at the bar, and walked out with Anna, had seemed eternal. Quinn had picked the twenty dollar bill up at the base of one of the stools, and handed it across to the bartender.

It was McCarthey who had given Quinn his name, called him "Mr. Quinn" and later just "Quinn" instead of "Terry," the name he had come to college with. McCarthey had given him liquor as if that were an ordinary thing, listened to his opinions, read his writing, and laughed at things that Quinn's father—the real Mr. Quinn—had said. "Worcester-wisdom," he had called it; and then he would always say, "But no worse than what we produce here in Boston," and laugh again.

Even though McCarthey had apologized a week or so later, Quinn stayed well out of his way from then on. McCarthey's wife left him, and he left the university after that year, went out to some school in Kansas, but Quinn didn't even hear about it until the following semester. Two years after that Quinn graduated and got a job with a pharmaceutical company in Chicago.

• • •

In the morning Quinn woke up late and when he went down for breakfast they had already stopped serving. So he drank coffee and read at the newspaper. The national pages were too grim, filled with killings and imbecilic cruelties, so he put the paper aside after a quick look at the sports pages. Must be Boston does this to me, he thought. Place is so contented. But I was never happy here. He used to say, Do something foolish; you'll feel better. Quinn laughed. Never was very good at that. Although I guess this stupid trip qualifies.

The waitress, a kid who looked about fourteen, with long red hair escaping its pins, came to the table with a steaming silver pitcher and filled his coffee cup. She smiled. "I can probably still get you some toast, if you like."

"No, thanks," Quinn said. "I'll get lunch later." He smiled back. "It's a nice place. Boston."

"We like it," the girl said. "Here on business?"

"Nope," Quinn said. "I guess I'm here to see someone. Find something I threw away."

She looked at him. "Well, maybe she still loves you," she said. "Happy New Year, anyway."

Quinn watched her walk away, left the newspaper and a tip, and walked outside for a cab. On the ride through town he didn't recognize anything, but farther out the dirty apartment buildings and little shops and broken streets started to at least look familiar. As the old taxi strained and bounced along Beacon Street, Quinn remembered leaving.

He had gotten the job late, in September, just about the time he had decided to give up and go back to Worcester, to his father's house. He had packed everything in three or four days and driven to Chicago in a sort of controlled panic, stopping overnight to see his family and then pushing on. He had not exactly forgotten the stuff up in the attic. It was a gallery of previous residents' detritus up there—dead black and white TV sets, and a lot of useless lamps, as he recalled. Things you couldn't just put in the trash, because they had come so dear—a television costs as much as a Bentley when you're a student—or because you couldn't understand how their powers had just evaporated, or because the attachment to them had been of such a personal character, like a love affair or friendship, that the objects deserved a ceremony, and there was no place to bury them. So you left them in the attic.

None or all of these reasons explained why Quinn had left the cardboard box up there. He'd been tired, and in a hurry, and even getting up into the attic was a gigantic hassle. And he had accepted his father's idea—to make a living, do something practical—even before the break with McCarthey.

By graduation, the year spent with the writer and his scruffy friends and his books and his praise had faded in memory. Even so Quinn still had to pretend to himself forgetting the box in the attic. The truth was by then he hated the damn book.

"Those people have very sad lives, Terry," his father had said. "They talk smart and never get paid very well."

To get up into the attic you had to shove a table or a chest of drawers underneath a small two-foot square opening in the ceiling, push the plywood panel out of the way, and hoist yourself up. Which is why Quinn assumed that now, eight years later, it was all still up there. If the house was still there, the stuff was still there.

Quinn had done, again, what his father suggested, and it had all worked out well. Better than that, actually—he could always lend a beloved ex-wife whatever she needed, or waste hundreds of dollars on a trip without blinking. The book, safely cottoned in memory, had faded like the other things, until the morning he had seen the notice in the paper that McCarthey had died.

He had been at his office, reading the Sunday paper on a Monday, and he saw the item about McCarthey and looked out at the white fog over the lake and thought, There but for the grace of God. It was like ten years he had not lived suddenly formed in his imagination, years of "disappointment" in some place like Kansas. He had looked out the big twenty-fourth floor window again, and McCarthey's voice came, 'No worse than hawking cold capsules in Chicago,' and Quinn had laughed.

• • •

"Hey," the cabdriver said. A black guy with no hair, who looked like Woody Strode. Quinn looked out.

The street seemed the same, kind of prim. The house

looked tiny, not the way Quinn had remembered it. The yard was mostly dirt and leaves, and the big oak tree between the porch and the street had now broken up the sidewalk completely with its roots. The fat limbs had been cut back cruelly, three or four feet from the trunk, so that the tree looked like a man with no hands, nine or ten half arms.

He paid the cabbie, walked up to the porch, pushed the button for the doorbell, and then looked at it. He'd heard no ring, so he knocked on the door, on the frame of the glass.

A young woman in jeans and a man's white shirt came. She pushed some black hair away her face and stood evaluating him for a minute before she drew the door open. "Yes?"

Quinn smiled. "Well," he said, smiling to beat the devil. "I'm Terry Quinn. I used to live here, a long time ago, in school. Are you a student?"

"I'm faculty," she said quickly, and then laughed. "Sort of faculty, I'm a lecturer. Students can't afford this place anymore. Neither can I for that matter. What can I do for you, Mr.—"

"Quinn," he said. "I left some stuff here. In the attic. And I wanted to see if it was still here. I can come back, if this is a bad time."

"Good a time as any," the woman said, and flipped her hair back again. "New Year's. I didn't know there was an attic. I've only been here a few months. Come in. Forgive the look of the place. My name's Teresa."

She had books everywhere, wandering along the baseboards and around corners back into the other rooms. Sheets over the windows and no furniture in the little front room except a desk with a small computer on it, and a chrome and wicker chair. Quinn stood looking at the single row of paperbacks marching the periphery of the floor.

She watched, sitting against a windowsill. "It's a joke," she said, waving toward the books. "Friend promised to build me some crackerjack bookshelves, but hasn't gotten around to it yet. He found me this house." Her green eyes flickered at him, and then at the room. "You look a little like him. Any good at bookshelves? So, where are you living now?"

Quinn shook his head. "Chicago," he said.

The woman laughed. Her hand went to her mouth, then to her hair again. "I don't think I'm tracking here," she said. "You came all the way from Chicago to Boston to get something out of my attic? Which doesn't exist? What is it? Rubies?"

"Actually it's some books and junk," Quinn said, and shrugged. "It's in the right hand bedroom, the attic. The door to it; it's a panel in the ceiling." He pointed back into the house, and shrugged again. "It's a particular book, a friend of mine wrote it. It's sort of a long story."

But when he told her about McCarthey, she recognized the name and, all of a sudden, lit up. "Let me call Ethan. God, he'd never forgive me. Another disciple. He'd love to talk to you." The telephone sat on the floor beside some papers and an ashtray. She settled on her haunches beside it and picked up the receiver. "Price you have to pay, if you want your memorabilia. You must have been here just about the same time he was." She flipped her hair, and then looked up. "Nervous habit," she said, and dialed. Quinn glanced around the small living room, trying to remember it.

"He knew there's an attic," she said, after she hung up the phone. "He knew your name, too. You sure you didn't know him when you were here?"

Quinn shook his head. "I don't remember."

The books lined the baseboards around the entire house, every room except the bathroom, like a popcorn string. There wasn't much furniture in the other rooms either. Her bed was a futon on the floor. When he pointed out the ceiling panel to her, she said, "I wondered what that was," and when he got into the attic, from an old steamer trunk on end that she had as a table, the low, dim space was empty. Quinn crouched and looked around at the flecks of dust in the stale air, wires looping out of the insulation and over ancient two-by-eights, their wood gone orange and brittle-looking.

"Well?" she said from down below.

"Nothing up here," Quinn said. "A lot of fiberglass and dust. Have you got a flashlight down there?"

She brought him a flashlight, handed it up to him, his hand grazing hers as he reached down without looking. Finally she put it in his fingers. But there wasn't anything in the attic, and Quinn could hardly breathe.

"I feel like an idiot," he said, when he got back down into the house. "I'm sorry to have bothered you."

"Are you all right?" she said.

"I feel weird," he said. "I haven't had anything to eat today. I'm a little light-headed. I mean, in addition to being addle-brained."

She laughed.

•   •   •

In the book on the title page, above his signature, McCarthey had written with a broad-tipped pen in black ink:

For Quinn—
   Smart money's on you. But smart people outsmart
   themselves.

126

Ethan did look like Quinn, but only a little. His coat was thin and ill-cut, and he had fine hair and quick eyes with dark circles around them, but otherwise he looked like a kid although they were about the same age. Looks like an athlete, Quinn thought, but he didn't really, he just seemed comfortable, at ease, especially around her, reaching out with his left hand, moving like a snake or something, and touching her wrist with the tip of a finger, intercepting her when she went to throw her hair back to the side of her head.

He had the book in his right hand. "I imagine this is what you're looking for," he said. "I found it last summer, before Teresa moved in. I've got the other books, too, out in my car. I threw the rest of the stuff out. I'm sorry. There were about nine TV sets up there, all broken," he said, and laughed. "But I got five bucks apiece for them."

Quinn realized that he was staring at them. He smiled. "Doesn't matter," he said, and took the book. The jacket was still perfect, but had faded so that what was once a glossy black was almost charcoal. There was a white line drawing of a saxophone on the front, the book was about a musician.

"Are you all right?" Ethan put his hand out, as if Quinn might fall down.

"Ethan's got a book coming out," Teresa said.

"Small press," Ethan said. "No big deal. Not much to show for ten years. But it keeps the dean happy. You must have known the old man pretty well. I had him for one course." He nodded to the book in Quinn's hand. "This isn't easy to come by, a first edition. I have another one, but mine's not signed. You remember the inscription?"

Quinn couldn't stop looking at him.

"He's starving to death," Teresa said. "He forgot to eat. We need to get him something to eat."

"I remember," Quinn said. "I remember it had a 'but' in it. Everything he ever said had a 'but' in it. I just didn't hear it. It wasn't the way I was raised."

He put the book back in Ethan's hand and watched him as he opened it, watched him as he read McCarthey's black script again, watched him as in the space of a minute's time he grew much older, gained weight, scratched for money, taught classes, had kids, wrote more books, suffered disappointments, drank, slept with women, made a thousand jokes, laughed, and did much that was foolish. Quinn liked him. "I'm glad I came," he said. "I'm glad to finally get a look at you." In the car Quinn said, "That's all I came for really."

Ask Again Later

This is my life, Zachary was thinking on Tuesday evening August 24, 2004, as he sat in the back of his office looking at the boarders, three cats and a sad looking half shepherd puppy. Slumped against one side of its cage, the puppy barely moved, just a little ripple in the fur above its eyes, staring at him. "Oh the poor little doggie," Zachary said. "Why don't you give it a rest? Let's consider the rest of your days. Eating rib eyes and bouncing around in some backyard, napping under the pines, pretty much the rest of your life." The dog watched him without blinking. The phone buzzed in the front office, and still the puppy stared.

"You probably think that's a customer—excuse me, a 'patient'—but you're wrong. That is Sandy Dean, calling to put me on TV. I saw some poor slob get stabbed to death, and so Sandy wants to talk to me. That's probably her secretary. Or somebody like that." He shrugged. The answering machine picked up and after a moment a man spoke, but Zach couldn't make out who it was or what was said. He looked at one of the cats, an old black with three legs and one good eye. The other eye was milky, opaque. "Right, Hector?" he said. "You know what's the matter with you, Hector? You believe in the social system. I mean, you don't believe in it, really, but you think they know best."

They hadn't caught the guy yet, and in a way Zach hoped they never did. He didn't want to testify, for one thing, and it wasn't as simple as that anyway. The guy that got stabbed—got killed—was a big guy, much bigger than the other one, and he was sort of asking for it, hassling the little guy, a bully. Zach had been trying to get himself to say something, trying to get himself to intervene, hoping that maybe just by walking into the situation he might stop it, before the little guy took care of it. Secretly, Zach was almost glad the other guy got his, though he wondered if he should feel that way. The guy was dead, after all. The little guy was "at large," they said.

Stephanie showed up in the little kitchen which adjoined the back room. "Zach," she said, "this is not the way to fame and fortune. How does the city's hot new veterinarian TV star spend his evenings? Moping in his office with sick kitties. See it all tonight at eleven." She had changed clothes, now in jeans and some kind of turtleneck shell or leotard, cream colored. She had dirty blonde hair and dark brows, a Waspy face, and beautiful eyes.

"Looking good," Zachary said. "Looking kinda gorgeous. Can we still say that? 'Gorgeous?' Not to an employee, huh?"

"It's after hours, you can say anything you want. In fact, I wish you would." She set her purse down on the white counter opposite the boarding cages. "I figured you'd still be here," she said, shaking her head.

"I'm unwinding," Zach said. He nodded at the black cat in the steel cage beside him. "Me and Hector. Decrepit old fuck." He shook his head. "It's all so creepy."

"So maybe you'll take me to dinner?" Stephanie said. "Something fancy? Red Lobster?"

"New shoes?" he said, pointing. The loafers she was wearing were violently shiny. "I like 'em. They look like Dodges."

She gave him a puzzled look.

"As in Chrysler Corporation." He nodded, looking around

the white room. Most of the cages were empty. Opposite on the wall above the white counter hung a four-color poster of a skeletal cat, with lines flaring away from each bone to a name at the periphery. The lines and the letters at the end of them were oddly thin, fine. "Chrysler shoes."

"Zach, why do you flirt with me all the damn time if you're not going to do anything about it?"

"You have an unrealistic world view," Zach said, and reached through the gray bars of the cage to stroke the matted fur of the cat's forehead. "One which I'd either have to support, or demonstrate its falsity. Either way, somebody'd wind up real unhappy. Either way, it's a lot of work."

"You miserable son of a bitch," she said, and swung at him, half heartedly, but with a closed fist. He caught her arm, and she swung around to face him.

"Hey, c'mon," he said, trying to steady her, stop her. "What're you doing? I was just kidding. Ow, shit," he yelled, as she bit him, hard, on the muscle curving up into his neck. "Goddamn, Stephanie." He grabbed his shoulder. She hooked her leg around his, and even though he was six inches taller and forty pounds heavier, threw him to the floor like it was nothing, barely breathing heavy.

On the floor Zach sighed, pinched his shoulder. "Jesus, you learn all that at the dojo, or something?" he said, and lay back on the white tile for a second before jerking up. "There're germs down here, Stephanie. It's filthy." He checked the floor on either side of him.

"C'mon. Breathe in, take a deep breath. That's alcohol and Clorox. The hypochondriac veterinarian. You're a mess, Zach." She sat down on the floor beside him, pulled his shirt collar aside to look at the bite. "Barely broke the skin."

"You're fired. Broke the skin?!" he said, craning his head to try to see and grabbing at the bite again with his fingers. "You broke the goddamn skin?"

"How're you going to explain that to Princess Anne?" But she was laughing, gently, at how hopeless he was. "You're a mess. You weren't kidding, were you? You really believe what you said—that garbage about my 'world view'—don't you?"

"I'm too old for you."

"Forty? Forty's too old for twenty-four?" She smirked, tossed her hair a little. "C'mon."

"Thirty-seven, and I'm involved. And you're twenty-five, not twenty-four." He laughed. "That's the stupidest lie I've ever heard, I think."

"You call that involved? Is she involved with you, or are you just involved with her? You're like two files that just happen to be in the same file cabinet."

He slid back across the floor and rested against the cabinet doors below the white counter. "Look. I am in love with you, how could I help it? But you believe you can make things happen by force of will. I know you can't. We're incompatible. You'd make me go bungee jumping and shit like that. Dancing. We're completely incompatible." He was shaking his head, slowly, looking at her. "Thanks for biting me, though."

"Oh, Jesus."

"What's the matter with that? A beautiful woman bites you, you appreciate it." He shrugged, shook his head again.

"I guess I'll run along then. When's the big interview?"

"After lunch. Two tomorrow afternoon," he said.

"Well, I'll see you in the morning." Stephanie got to her feet, looked into the cat's cage. "So what are your plans for tonight, Gramps? You and old Hector gonna go to a big bingo game? Play some dominos or something? What are you going to do about him anyway? Isn't it unethical to keep him? Hey kitty," she said, petting Hector with her fingers through the wire mesh.

"I'm a very ethical guy," Zach said. "Even when they're somebody else's ethics. Did we charge her for... him?"

Stephanie smoothed the already smooth fabric of her top, drawing her hands gently across her stomach. "No, we never charged her," she said. "But the old woman thinks he's deceased. A month ago."

"I just can't," Zach said, watching her from the floor. "He's not in pain, really, I don't think. Glaucoma, but the betoptic controls that. Just lame and half-blind."

"And emaciated and incontinent," she said.

"A little. What, you want me to put him down? Really?"

She looked at him quickly. "No, of course not. But he can't live in this goddamn cage. He'll get sick back here anyway. Won't the princess let you bring him home?"

Zachary cleared his throat.

"Sorry," Stephanie said. "That was a real womanish thing to say. Forgive me doctor for I have sinned." She feigned a deep sigh. "If you'll take me home with you, I promise to sin again and again."

"Please stop. You can't imagine how bad it makes a man feel to turn down—I mean, really bad."

She walked out of the back room into the hall leading to the reception area and the front door. "What I don't like about this, Zach, is the feeling I'm getting that you think you're protecting me. It's sort of paternalistic and arrogant and insulting. And old-fashioned." She walked away.

"I'm an old-fashioned guy," Zach called down the hallway. The front door slammed. "You think I want to be like this?" he shouted.

He stayed almost another hour and a half, talking to the

animals, watching the TV in the reception area, avoiding going home. The telephone message was a police officer. They had a suspect. It was urgent that Zach call back. He hoped it wasn't the pale boy whose terrified face he'd seen, a turn and a look, just before the run for the alley at the other end of the parking lot. Finally he closed up the office, drove home, and went to bed.

• • •

The next day, Zach was home from the office and ready at noon. They were coming for his interview at two o'clock, Sandy Dean had said. He sat by the big windows in the upstairs bedroom, not looking at the cardboard boxes stacked against one wall, neatly sealed, a green plastic dispenser of brown tape resting on the topmost box. His beard was trimmed, his Italian shirt pressed, and his eyes were getting flooded with Murine on the quarter hour.

Zach was supposed to talk about the stabbing. It had happened in the long, narrow parking lot that ran beside Lester's, a bar he liked downtown. He had been walking to his car, eleven o'clock at night, two guys arguing.

He looked out the window, down at the sidewalk. Across the street a man walked out the gate and onto the sidewalk, briskly, irritatingly certain of the importance of whatever errand he happened to be on. He was tall and thin, well-dressed in a dark gray suit, swinging his arms like a puppet. The suit looked shiny in the noonday sunlight. Zach watched him reach the corner and stop. "Now… look at your watch," Zach said. But the man stood looking at the traffic light. There was no traffic in the street. "Look at your watch," Zach said, and the man jerked his left arm, as if shooting his cuff, and checked his watch. Zach sat back away from the window and nodded. Just like the movie, he thought. I'm watching like in a movie, and he's imitating a busy guy in a movie.

While he was waiting for Sandy Dean and the TV people, he was also waiting for Anna to get off work at the restaurant so they could continue the argument that they'd been having in all their free time for the past two weeks, ever since she had told him that she was moving out. She pretended to be jealous of him and Stephanie, pretended to believe they were sleeping together. But she was really mixed up with someone she had met at the restaurant and spent most of her time out with the restaurant people who spent all their time doing dope and bar-hopping. She was a manager at the restaurant, so she could do pretty much what she wanted and she had promised to be home before the TV people got there.

Zach wasn't innocent exactly. He had slept with a woman, one of his customers, who had a big house in Berkshire Heights. Twice. He had told Anna about it, though now he regretted it. It all happened six months ago, and though it was easy, even sweet, it was over. The woman helped make it work, that's what he couldn't get Anna to understand, all he had to do was show up. She was relaxed. If he said, I've got to go home to my girlfriend, she said, "Sure." He hadn't yet told Anna that even though the woman was forty, she was an extremely tasty, sexy woman with a soft little belly and sharp breasts like a girl. That the woman was funny and oddly kind. "Generous" was the word he had settled on.

He wanted Anna home before the TV people showed up. He wanted somebody else on his team. He had felt like a shmuck the night it happened, standing around while the police and the television crews went about their work.

Other people had been in the parking lot that night and one of them called the cops on a car phone. A guy named Dick Connant had gotten all the attention at the time, a loud-mouth who really hadn't seen much of anything. He told the cops the little guy looked Mexican. That the guy was old. That the guy got into a car... uh, I think it was some kind of four wheel drive. None of that was true. The little guy was blond, young, ran on foot. The cops were oddly uninterested in Zach, when he had tried to tell them what he had seen. To be fair, they weren't very interested in Dick Connant's story, either. But he had been all over the TV for two nights.

The other guy, the dead one, had worked at a machine shop. Zach didn't know what exactly a "machine shop" was, except that that was where they send brake discs to be "turned"—ground smooth—things like that. It wasn't like he was really dead, he hadn't been dead the last time Zach had seen him, when they trussed him up and wheeled him into the ambulance waiting in the alley at the end of the parking lot. "Dead" was something they said on television. The guy across the street in the shiny suit was "dead." Dead. Zach almost didn't believe it. But it was beginning to get to him.

There wasn't any music, he thought, watching the street from his window, looking for Anna. In movies, there's always lots of music. He had seen fights, even been in fights, in school, and they were usually clumsy and often short. This one had been like that. He had never even seen the knife, just the two guys clinch and then the big guy fall back and the other guy run. Took fifteen seconds, tops. And now the guy's dead? He shook his head.

"What're you doing?" Anna said, from the doorway.

"I was waiting for you," Zach said. "I didn't see you come up the street."

"I've been downstairs for twenty minutes," she said, small, blonde, with shining blue eyes. She was still wearing the black slacks and white tuxedo shirt from the restaurant. "When do the TV people get here? Two?"

"Yeah, I thought they'd be here by now."

"Zach, it's one-thirty."

"One thirty-five," he said, nodding toward the clock on the bedside table.

"Have you thought about what we talked about the other night? I don't want to lose you, as a friend, I mean, but I don't want to go on this way, either." Smiling, she looked to him particularly beautiful in the midday light passing in the big windows, clear and edged by the whiteness lent them by the thin curtains pulled back to the sides of each. "I move in with Mary and Marianne next Friday," she said. "The first." She watched him, waiting for a protest, and when she didn't get any, turned and walked out of view down the hall.

They didn't come until four. There was Sandy Dean, who looked enough like the sea of blonde anchorwomen on the networks to pass at a small local news operation, and three men, the two with the camera and the sound equipment who looked like kids, and a third guy, older, who basically stood around and did nothing, looked at the furniture and a framed photograph Anna had on the wall, a picture of ice cubes on a white enamel surface, melting.

"Don't be nervous," Sandy Dean had said, in the little preparatory session they had sitting together on the couch in the living room, before going outside to "shoot." She patted his forearm gently, and smiled. It was hard not to like her, and Zach didn't try. The light was easier to handle outside, she said, as long as it wasn't too bright, and it wasn't too bright this afternoon. "You're a veterinarian?" she said. "That's great.

I wanted to be a vet when I was little girl, I really did. But you know, I got interested in journalism. Did you know the two men that were fighting in the alley?"

"Parking lot," Zach said. "No, I didn't know them. I was just leaving, getting my car."

"Where did you go to vet school? Cornell?"

"You did want to be a veterinarian, didn't you?" Zach said, and Sandy Dean laughed. He liked her laugh. "No, I went to Texas A & M. They've got an awful good school down there, too."

"They sure do," Sandy Dean said. "When we go outside, just talk to me, pretend the other people aren't there. And think happy thoughts. The camera magnifies everything and a frown'll make you look like Ebenezer Scrooge on the tape." She cocked her head to the side and made a big clown frown at him. Then she laughed. "C'mon, sugar, let's make some news," she said, standing up.

Zach stood up, and following her outside, he saw a look pass from her to the guy who was inspecting the furniture, an instant in which her entire personality seemed to fall away and she looked as if she was thinking, I hate this job.

The interview itself took ten or fifteen minutes. Zach thought about setting things straight, but finally he only suggested that he wasn't certain that the guy was young and Mexican-American. Sandy Dean wasn't interested in his doubts and the more diffident his answers got, the more she suggested maybe the police or the medical technicians had not or were not handling the matter very well. Whatever she was looking for, he wasn't supplying it, which on a moment's reflection seemed like the best way to proceed, especially if you might have to explain yourself to cops later on. So he gave a dull interview, and even though he felt like a failure, especially after she had been so charming and schmoozy earlier, he didn't have to worry about it. He even said to Anna, after Sandy and the others had packed their gear and left, "If I get thirty seconds on the news, I'll be surprised."

• • •

He went back by the office at five to check on things, happy to find Stephanie still there.

"The old man has a little business in his bad eye," she said from her chair behind the high reception counter which cut off the back third of the room. She was watching television. Only the very top of her head was visible, her streaky brown and yellow hair. "Hector? He's got a little infection, I think."

"Did you put some antibiotic in it?"

"From a tube," she said.

"That's what I meant," Zach said, and shuddered. "What did you think I meant, an injection?" He walked back and around the counter; it was a baseball game on WGN, a Cubs game. "How can you watch that?" he said. "It's soporific."

"Used to be good, when they had the Hawk. Andre Dawson, he was a coiled spring. A natural phenomenon. Like bacon, or something. That Astros guy—Bagwell—he has a little something of the old Andre, but not really. So, how did your interview go? It took three hours?"

"I think you're wonderful," Zach said. He watched her slow turn, her lowered brows. He could feel the dumb look on his face.

"Pardon me?" she said.

"Nothing," Zach said. "Nevermind," he said, and took the

second chair. "They did that in school, stuck needles in their eyes." He shuddered. "I hate baseball. Every bore in the world likes baseball. You don't like baseball, do you?"

"I'm only in it for the beefcake." She shook her head. "There was a call from that cop, Officer Hodge." She drew herself up in a military bearing and mocked his voice: "'This is Officer Hodge; make my day.' He was a little insistent. Are you avoiding him?"

"Of course I'm avoiding him. He's the fucking police. Look, the way I see it, one guy was behaving really badly and the other guy finally couldn't stand it anymore. I'm supposed to be Mr. Good Citizen and send him to Raiford for life?"

"Okay, okay. All right. You also got a frantic call from Mrs. Hochstetter. She's afraid to feed it at all. You were a little hard on her. So pussy's a little chubby, so what? What are you laughing about?"

"It's—When I was working for Dr. Warren, he used to have people bringing in these cats worrying about how they'd lost their appetites and he'd pull a serious face and say he'd need to keep them for a couple days. So he'd just not feed the cat at all, he'd starve it, and then he'd say—" Zach was laughing. "—he'd say, 'That cat'll be so hungry when they get it home, it'll tear a leg off the dining room table...' And then he'd just laugh and laugh." He caught himself, shrugged. "You asked me what I was laughing about."

"Is it time for your interview?" Stephanie looked around and found the remote control, cut to a local channel.

"I don't think Peter Jennings is going to run it," Zach said. "I don't think it'll be on at six, either. She didn't even show up till four o'clock. Maybe at eleven."

"We'll watch it at my place," Stephanie said.

He just stared at her bright eyes for a moment, thinking

in a vague way of what his life had been like twenty years earlier, when he was a teenager, remembering what it was like to spend every moment thinking about women, girls, one particular woman, one particular girl.

"Great," she said. "Should I get dip?"

Zach shook his head. "Sorry," he said. "I'm sorry. It's too much."

She had turned back to the television, her jaw and her shoulders set, her eyes narrowed. "Yeah, yeah, sure," she said, and shrugged.

"Stephanie…"

"I've got to get going," she said. She stood up and started straightening the desk below the high counter. "You should call Mrs. Hochstetter and let her off the hook. She's sure the cat is headed for renal failure. Tonight. Stress on the kidneys, you know." She swung around, barely missing him with an elbow, and walked out from behind the counter and over to the door. "Good night, Zach," she said, and left.

"Stephanie," he said, softly, watching the big door swing closed behind her.

Zach called the cop and was surprised that he was still there. He had to come down and identify the suspect, and he had to do it this evening. Zach tried to ask some questions but Officer Hodge only asked him if he could get there in twenty minutes.

• • •

Zach had been to a police station in another town once long before, when he had to give them fingerprints to get a taxi license. He had driven a cab for a while when he was an undergraduate, a lot of taking very poor people to cash welfare checks and very old people to supermarkets, people who couldn't afford or couldn't control cars. And once also long ago, he had picked Anna up outside this police station, after she'd been arrested for shoplifting. They had gotten a lawyer and he made the thing disappear, charged a hundred dollars or so. It was bewildering how easily it evaporated. Nothing ever happened the way it did on television, or in books.

But he'd never been inside this one before. The building was a big long rectangle with a ten foot ceiling, mostly open space. Zach asked two people who didn't know who Officer Hodge was before finding a woman who did, who made a telephone call and then said he wasn't there. But whoever the woman was talking to told her that Zach should wait. The woman wasn't wearing a uniform. She was young, with a dark complexion, probably an Arab, pretty enough but with slightly protruding eyes. She pointed to a chair.

"Someone will be with you," she said. And then when he didn't move, "Sit down."

Zach sat. He hadn't anticipated waiting. There was nothing to look at beside the woman and he didn't want to look at her so he looked around at the furniture, a few desks and some polished aluminum chairs like the one he was sitting in, a burlap-covered room divider with things pushpinned to it, a picture of an old woman with glasses and white hair, a picture from the newspaper of two TV cops with their guns held high, pointed at the picture of the old woman.

Zach looked at the floor. Scratched white linoleum. Waiting. What am I doing here, he thought.

The Arab woman got up from behind her desk and started toward some double doors in the back wall of the big room, limping. One of her legs was markedly shorter than the other.

She was wearing a stylish, close fitting black skirt. She pushed through the doors and they swung back. From somewhere came the sound of a police radio, and from somewhere else the sound of a fat man, laughing.

Zach felt wrong, queasy, out of balance. Hector's dying, he thought. He's going to die. He's dying now. I didn't put him down, but I put him in a cage. The halfass kind of thing I always do. He shook his head. It occurred to him to jump up and run out of the building, run to his car, drive back to the office, and see. I'm losing it, he thought. Hector is fine. Hector is okay. Like a thief in the night. Nothing ever happens the way you expect it. He looked around, but there was no one, so he looked back down at the linoleum.

The double doors swung in, and a short, balding blond guy in a suit came in and walked over. "Dr. Zachary?" he said. "I'm Detective Welch."

Zach stood up, and took the man's hand, shook it. "No, Zachary's my first name. Zachary Thomas."

"A pleasure," the cop said. He was a smiley guy, sure of himself. "Could you come with me?"

He led Zach through the door and up a stairway to a room on the second floor where seven or eight men and one woman stood and sat here and there in a room about half the size of the lower floor. One of the men was the pale blond boy from the parking lot that Zach had seen four days earlier.

"See anybody you know?" Welch said, happy.

Zach looked sharply away from the boy and back at Welch, with an uncomprehending expression on his face which made no impression on the cop, who looked back down at a piece of paper.

"That's the way Hodge has it in his notes—Dr. Zachary.'" He grinned. "He's only working with fifteen watts, if you

143

know what I mean. Could you wait here a minute?" he said, getting up. Then he walked all the way across the room and out a door opposite the door they had come in.

Smug little shit, Zach thought. It's one thing to be a big guy and push people around, but it's even worse to be a little guy. A little guy should know better.

Zach looked around at the boy, who was sitting fifteen feet away in a burnished aluminum frame chair like the ones downstairs, like all the chairs. He was facing straight ahead, occasionally glancing this way or that, like a kid at a party to whom no one was speaking. He didn't seem to recognize Zach, even though he looked right at him a couple of times. He looked frightened, doomed, the same way he had looked that night in the parking lot. But now he has us shoving him and slapping his face, Zach thought.

Welch came back into the room with another guy in a suit, a tall guy with a pock marked face. He was chewing gum. "Well?" Welch said.

Zach blinked. "Well what?" he said.

The cops looked at each other. "Do you see anybody that you know?" Welch said, slowly, with menace in his voice.

Involuntarily, Zach began shaking his head.

"What do you say?" Welch said.

Zach shook his head. "I thought I was supposed to look at a line-up or something," Zach said.

The cops snorted. "Maybe you'd like a guest spot on *Geraldo*, too," Welch said. "Or a maybe a ride with O.J." He put a hand on the back of Zach's chair, slipped into a half crouch beside it, lifted his other hand and uncurled a finger to point across at the pale boy sitting terrified. "You see that kid? Is that the kid you saw in the parking lot the other night?" He was pointing at the boy, but looking at Zach.

"No," Zach said. "No, that's not him. He was older, and sort of dark." Zach took a deep, loud breath.

Welch looked at the pock marked guy, then back at Zach. He flicked his coat open. There were handcuffs shining on his belt. "What are you saying, doctor?"

"It's not him," Zach said, shrugging, stifling a smile. "I'm sorry."

Welch straightened up. "We're going to get him anyway, doctor," he said. He waved a hand, dismissing him.

• • •

Zach drove past his apartment and on to the office. His heart was galloping a little in his chest. It was about nine-thirty when he let himself in and turned on all the lights; it always felt creepy in the office at night in the dark. I want a drink, he thought. I'm so tired of doing what I should do.

There was beer in the small refrigerator in the office kitchen in the back, but he took a bottled water instead. It felt creepy with the lights on, too, like he was too visible, so he turned them off in the front and sat in the dark. After a while he went back to the boarding cages. Hector was still alive, just asleep.

Zach woke the old cat up to bring him out front and set him on the desk behind the reception counter and sat in Stephanie's chair, but with his feet up to block the cat from jumping from the desk. Hector wasn't inclined. He lay where he had been put and went back to sleep. As Zach sat in the dark, glancing at the telephone, thinking about her, it was almost as if he was breathing her presence in and out, thinking, remembering being seventeen, watching the tall red numbers on the digital clock at the edge of the desk registering later and later, trying to quiet his breathing. She's what I want, he thought, picking up the phone. I might as well start it.

Hush Hush

When Paulie, on her way to her interview with the arts people, had stopped by his office at the bank, she laughed and said, "Tilden, when're you going to move in?" He had ignored it, but now he agreed.

His office was dull, as dull as people had always said it was the first time they saw it. The first six months he had left it as he had found it, the shelves empty, the walls bare. Wooden coat rack in front of the windows. But it drew so many comments and strange looks that he had taken a weekend and moved all the furniture around; everybody else was always doing that. Then he bought Mexican rugs for the walls and, for the table, marketing and shelter magazines which when they were superseded each month moved to tidy stacks on the shelves. Got rid of the damn coat rack.

Still they told him it was dull, and although he thought their offices no more interesting than his—Loeffler's MOMA calendars and butterfly chairs—he now agreed with them about his own. Dull. Maybe a two-headed secretary out front. But where would Kelli sit? Where would she put her cat snapshots and dead seashells? Maybe some posters, for some television religion or a fifth-rate rock group, one he had never heard or heard of, which wouldn't be hard to find, as he never listened to the radio anymore or watched the music channels or turned on the stereo for that matter. Silence, Tilden thought, was sweet, like Saturday mornings had been.

The Saturday that Paulie had first arrived at his door, he had ignored her knock, sat beside the plants sipping coffee in the slanting light from the mini blinds over the windows, but she would not go away, so he finally got up and went to the door and opened it, then stood there denying he was her father, she, who should have been more embarrassed than he was, because she was outside and he was inside, just as adamantly, one foot up on a suitcase, asserting it.

He had shut the door on her, at least twice, then looked out through the blinds in the vain hope that she'd go away. She was tall, nearly six feet, muscular, dark-haired, Italian. Jeans and khaki shirt. She had settled on the top step and lit a cigarette, coughed, then, after five minutes or so, knocked again.

"Tilden," she said, through the door. "This is silly. You think you can ignore me and I'll go away? I've got no place to go." More knocking. "Nineteen sixty-six. Boston. My mother's name was Tina. You were drunk. You made a big thing about never drinking anything but vodka. Stupid, right? But what can you expect from a twenty year old? You had a show on the college radio station; you played Doors records, over and over. You have a big scar across the back of your neck. They took off a birthmark or something. Let me in."

It had ruined his morning, and all the mornings since, because now she was up before seven every day, with the blinds open and coffee brewing, like one of those women in the ads on the Weather Channel, leaping out of bed, where she had somehow mysteriously washed her face—there was never any oil on it—and her nightgown unwrinkled, so that he wondered if she had slept in it at all. He had been married twice, and women just didn't look like this in the morning, and their voices weren't light and had no lilt, and their eyes were bleary. Like his own. But Paulie came out of the back bedroom of the small apartment new born, every morning. It was misery.

One Friday, before leaving for work, she said, "Still don't like me, do you?" and he had said, "You get in my way," and then he had thought about it all day at the office.

When he got home, she wasn't there yet, so he went to the market around the corner and bought a loaf of his bread, and a jar of his brand of peanut butter, and two rib eyes, meat, and a case of Schaefer, which he counted on to have all the additives and unnatural junk which she claimed gave her headaches. He was arranging it all on the kitchen counter when she got back.

"Where've you been?"

"What's all this stuff?" she said, throwing her hair back with her hand. "Steaks, no less. You're showing the flag, right? That's so cute!"

"Where have you been?"

"Had to work late. Some very important cultural stuff happening next week, some kind of meeting. I met this very sexy British guy. His name is Ryan. Only he's short. Comes to here," she said, drawing a hand across her breasts. "If you didn't want me to work late, you shouldn't have gotten me a job."

"Does this little guy have a little apartment?"

"You mean," she said, "a little apartment I could move into? Let's not rush things. I only just met him. When do we eat?"

They ate the steaks—he cooked—and then drank the entire case of beer, save one, until to her, the headache she planned became somehow uproariously funny, and to him, she began to look more like a woman, and less like a problem, or at least like a different kind of problem, until he was shaking his head, mostly to stop looking at her, stop noticing how pretty and how perfect she was, like the pretty, perfect vegetables she brought home from the natural store, or her sweet breath which he knew came from some kind of natural toothpaste she got at the same place.

He got up and walked from the front room into the kitchen, and opened the refrigerator. "You want this?" he said, holding the last can of Schaefer up in the triangle of light from the refrigerator, above the door.

She shook her head. "You're jealous, aren't you?" she said. "Of Ryan? You don't want your daughter going——"

"Oh no," he said. "I've gotten rid of two wives. I'm not going to have a daughter. The price is too high." And that ended the party.

She stopped, blinked, looked at him, then started to cry, quietly.

"I'm going to sleep," he said. "I'm sorry. You forced your way in here. I got you a job. I had a nice, quiet, sensible life, before. Peaceful, goddamn it. I pay the rent. I like you, but…"

"But?"

"I'm going to sleep," he said. "There's one more can of beer. On the top shelf. And some bourbon in the cabinet. And I sleep all day Saturday, so if you get up at the crack of dawn, don't start playing the radio and singing, for God's sake." He looked at her. "Tiptoe, for God's sake. Understand?" He looked away, and walked back to his bedroom and took his clothes off and got into bed, and fell asleep before he could get angry. She was right; he was jealous, but only a little. It would pass.

• • •

The next morning, he woke up at eleven, with a headache. When he got to the front of the apartment the glare from the windows hurt. He closed the blinds, twisting one of the plastic wands until he felt it break up at the top behind the sheet metal where you couldn't see what was going on. He thought, briefly, of going to the other windows and breaking the other two, on purpose, but let it go, settled down into the couch.

"Aspirin?" she said, from the kitchen.

He nodded.

When she brought him the pills and a glass of water, she was decked out in high heels and a long rayon dress, black, all open lace over a black slip, or a bodystocking, or something. "Anything else you want?"

He squinted and blinked. "What is this?" he said, waving his hand at her clothes.

"This is the Forties look. You like it?"

"On Saturday?" he said. "Anyway, I thought high heels were unnatural. A chauvinist conspiracy or something."

She gave him a blank look, and then said, "I need the car. Okay? I'm not walking nineteen blocks looking like this. I have to go in today. Big project." When she saw his squinting, smug expression, she said, "I'm going to work because Ryan will be there and I put on some stuff because Ryan will be there, fancy stuff, this dress, the stockings. I feel stupid enough without you staring at me." She stood looking at him. "Why're you shaking your head?"

He smiled. "I'm remembering the years I spent worrying about whether women cared about me, noticed me. The work they must have been doing that I never saw." He shut his eyes.

"If it's non-effective, I'll put my soviet outfit back on. If it's—"

"It's effective," he said. "Maybe too effective. Just make sure old Ryan's got a nice apartment."

"I told you last night. He lives in a hotel."

He nodded. "I figure about twenty minutes for the aspirin to work. Ten more minutes."

"Tilden? Tell me something." She picked her purse out of the seat of the armchair at the end of the couch, stood pushing things around in the purse until she came up with a tiny maroon brush. She drew it slowly through her long, dark hair. "Why do you live this way?"

There was a time when a woman brushing her hair was the most beautiful thing in the world to him. "This way?"

"In the dark," she said.

"I'm a mole," he said, and pointed to his eyes.

"Don't you ever want to dance? Or go to a movie or—Or a woman? People die, you know? Then it's over. I mean, you bought a brown car, for God's sake. Mama—She told me you used to be brash. What happened?" She dropped the hairbrush back into the purse and zipped it, put her hands on her hips. "All you do is work and eat. And sleep."

"I drink."

"Not very much," she said. "Never enough."

"If you drink too much, you have to think about it." He looked up, but the light still hurt. "The car keys are on the hook, by the door." Squinting.

"Yeah, I got them." She shook her head, opened the purse again. "I've gotta go." She leaned over him and gently kissed his hair. "I could stay home. We could drink up the bourbon. Go to bed."

"Get out!"

"Just kidding, Tilden, Jesus. Calm down. You're acting like my father or something." He lifted his feet up on the couch and turned to face the back, heard the purse zip closed again, and then her heels on the hardwood floor, finally the spring slip the bolt into the latch of the door.

• • •

Paulie was gone all day, and all day Sunday. Some time during the night she had returned the car, because when he looked out the blinds on Sunday morning, there it sat in front of the building. Brown.

He tried not to wait for her, even tried *Sixty Minutes* after the football games were over, but got distracted trying to tell whether the newsmen's suits were expensive, and their watches and their haircuts. He even thought of trying to call the hotel—but then remembered that he didn't know the kid's last name. He used to read, but that was no good either, he couldn't concentrate, so finally he got out the vacuum cleaner.

He straightened the rugs, pushed the chairs and the couch around, and ran the old vacuum back and forth, sweating, until the plug jerked out of the wall and he moved it to a new outlet. He left her room until last, stood before the door for a minute, and finally pushed open the door. The floor was littered with coathangers and panties, khaki shirts, sections of newspapers and crisp department store bags, leg weights, running clothes, and small balls of black hair. Tilden let the hose drop, walked over and sat on her unmade bed. He could smell Shalimar, or Emeraude, one of those.

There had been a girl, before he left school the first time, in Boston, a pretty, quiet Italian so shy she could barely speak. He remembered riding her bicycle into an old church, sitting

up by the altar. "I'm the bishop. You're the bishop's whore."
He put his hand to the back of his neck, touched the scar.
Vodka, that was right. The time he had gotten beat up on
Marlborough Street, for taking somebody's liquor, she took
care of him, covered his face with hot wet towels, touched his
forehead, and brought him aspirin for three days. "I don't believe it," he said, out loud, and looked at the floor, settling for
a moment on her discarded underwear, then quickly looking
at the vacuum in the doorway.

Tilden stood up, and then sat back down, looking at a
Vogue on top of a stack of magazines. He thought the telephone was ringing, in the front of the apartment, but listening
harder, heard nothing. Jesus, he thought, no thank you.

The girl on the magazine cover, blonde, in a three-quarter
pose, her perfect face disappearing under the logo and her soft
breasts nearly bare above a pale blue evening dress, holding his
eyes, spaghetti straps, that's what they used to call them, ten
years since he'd done this, looked at the goddamn pictures so
hard it was as if you were trying to make the photograph start
breathing, and he remembered knowing their names, Renee
Russo, and Lois what's her name, and Kim Alexis, and Lauren
Hutton, of course, Verushka, way back, and Karen Graham...

"Fuck this," he said, shoving the magazines off onto the
floor so that they slid over the clothes and hangers all the way
to the wall. Tilden lay back on the bed, but when he felt his
shoulders touch the sheet, jerked back up onto his elbows,
then sat straight up and grabbed the clock from the table and
threw it against the wall, and then, for good measure, finding
nothing else, threw the table the clock had been on and picked
up magazines from the floor and threw them too, tearing the
covers, listening to the pages slap against each other until they
hit the walls.

I am enjoying this, he thought, and looked at the radio, on the carpet. I am enjoying this very much. He brought his shoe down on the imitation wood grain plastic, in which there was a little too much black, and it only sort of squeaked, so he stepped back to kick it into the wall, getting a little lift so that it hit about two feet up from the floor molding, leaving a black dent in the paint and loose plastic below. "Up, and… good!" He was almost shouting, twisting around, turning back, looking, and he tried the bed, with both hands managing to throw the mattress against the other wall, a spinning throw which let him fall, like a dancer, on top of the box spring where he lay looking up, gasping for breath. This is it, he thought. This is the way I used to be. He laughed and looked around. Standing in the doorway, her feet in carefully chosen spots in the pretzel formed by the hose of the vacuum cleaner, Paulie was looking back at him, smiling.

"You taking a break or what?" she said.

He started giggling, watching her, staring at her, the black dress which was all holes, black faded to a sort of charcoal color, her hip cocked, her pelvis pushed front and center by the high heels like the models in the magazines, staring, and he could feel the look on his face, just past a smile, enjoying it, drunk with love, or something like love, thinking, I'm giggling, for God's sake, like everybody else.

"Tilden? Are you okay? Should I call somebody?" He blinked. "You hurt," he said, "you know, just standing there in that goddamn dress. But… don't move. Are you tired?"

She stood, motionless, like a woman on display with her perfect brown eyes, perfect black hair, and glowering dark skin wrapped around the muscles of her neck. "Now?!" she said, reading his eyes. "Now you want to fuck?"

"No…" Tilden shut his eyes. "Yes. I wish you hadn't said

it that way. We could break some more stuff instead," he said. "Let's do that." He got up, reached down for one of the pastel blue leg weights, hesitated, and picked up the radio, the cord wrapping itself around his leg until he kicked loose and reached out with it, saying, "Yeah. Here. You go first. I'm buying." He handed her the radio, which, missing only a couple of the clear plastic lenses from the front, felt like a brick.

She kicked her shoes into the room and stood weighing the radio in her hand, taking practice throws, sidearm.

"Hard," Tilden said. "Throw it hard. It's a tough little bastard." He leaned over, kissing her neck just as she threw. The radio hit the opposite wall and fell apart.

"Good," Tilden said. "That was good. Great. Sorry about…"

"It's okay," she said. "It felt… nice. How much shit can we break?"

"A prudent amount."

She rolled her eyes. "You're buying?"

He nodded. "Get the bourbon," he said, and then followed her as she walked down the hall, her long arms stretched out so that her hands slid along the walls tearing the Jazz Festival posters in half leaving meandering white edges which looked like the stock charts the newspapers published. She rose up on her toes to slap the sickly beige cover off the smoke alarm, which immediately began howling. In the living room she pushed over a lamp, and Tilden stepped on the shade until the bulb shattered inside. She cleared a bookshelf, hooked her stockinged foot under the table in front of the couch, lifted it a quarter inch, and yelped. Turned around, picked up books from the carpet. "Here," she shouted, handing him one, pointing at the three plants under the window, and then they threw books, one by one, until the plants were down. She turned and put her arms around his neck, sagging against him, pulling him down. "Tilden," she said, lips to his ear to be heard above the screaming smoke alarm, wrapping herself around him, "let's break a rule." He reached down, put his hands on her, feeling her through the dress, and felt like he was all hands.

• • •

"Tilden?" she said, in the morning, leaning over him, in the nightgown although she had slept without it, standing now with a cup of coffee in her hand, finger marks up and down her bare arms, her eyes clear, her hair shining, brushed to within an inch of its life. "You've gotta get up."

Sitting up in the bed, he set the coffee aside, and drew his fingers along her forearm. "Me?"

She nodded, sat beside him. "I bruise easily," she said, and grinned. "I was always very proud of that. If you say you're sorry, I'll break your face." She looked at her arms, and the grin turned to a broad smile. "I mean, I'd rather you didn't."

"I'm sorry."

She looked at him.

"How bad is it out there?" he said, pointing out the bedroom door. "The furniture. It's all coming back to me."

She shook her head. "Minor league," she said. "I've already put most of it back. I put that ugly plant in some water, in a mayonnaise jar. You're going to need a new lamp though. You can probably replace that one for a buck and a half."

"The lady has never bought a lamp."

"The gentleman has never been to the Salvation Army store."

"Right," he said. He put his hands on her breasts, felt her nipples through the thin nylon.

"Work," she said.

"Screw work."

"Tilden, you devil. You're going to break another rule?"

"Hey," he said, "there's only one rule. Jesus said. And then there're a lot of second-rate types making up a lot of extras. Middle management types. And Jesuits." He drew his hands away. "You in love with this Ryan person?"

"You mean, Did I sleep with him?"

He laughed. "No, I meant what I said." He kissed her through the nightgown, pulled away, smiled at her. "I assumed you screwed the child's brains out. Isn't that what you young people do?"

"That's it," she said. "I mean when we aren't snorting, shooting, smoking, dropping, popping, or tearing the wings off angels. Or stealing stuff or—"

"Hush," he said. "Hush hush."

She looked at him.

"It's a song. Was a song. When were you born, what year?" He shook his head. "Nevermind. In olden times this blues guy, Jimmy Reed, I think he lived in Dallas—He played harmonica and guitar and he had this trashy blues voice, we played him on the radio. A song called 'Hush Hush.' It was about noise. How there was too much noise. Sort of wonderful."

"I don't know whether I'm in love with him or not. Too soon to tell. He wants me to move in."

"A girl's got to find out, I guess." Tilden lay back in the bed, watching her.

"It was nice, last night, I mean throwing things and the rest of it, mostly the rest of it. I mean, I loved it. I mean, you. But look—" She was drawing circles in the sheet with her finger.

"Look. When I was about six Mama gave me a picture, this glossy picture, of you, of my father." She smiled, shook her head. "That picture was my favorite thing for about six years. You signed it. When I was about twelve, a girl told me it was Jim Morrison. The singer." She shrugged. "So I need another picture, see? Girl needs a picture."

"Let me get this straight," Tilden said. "Somehow you knew my—"

"Mama gave it to me. Your name? I got it from Mama."

"Okay. Anyway—"

"And Boston is right, and Baltimore, you living in Baltimore. There is a scar on the back of your neck, I've seen it. You want blood tests and shit? Paternity?"

"I want you not to be my kid. I like looking at you. Only not like you look at a daughter."

"There're lots of people to look at." She stood up, reached her hand up and split her hair between her fingers. "I've gotta go to work. You know Tilden, you're really fucked up," she said, and walked out of the room.

He looked toward the empty doorway. "Now!" he shouted. "I am now!"

But she didn't answer. He thought of getting up, of following her into the room and talking some sense into her, but when he imagined her shoulder in his hand, his face red and words spewing out in the southern accent which he fell into when he got angry, cared too much, the image reminded him of the bruises all over her arms, made him recall that he really didn't know what to say, that two women he had married and loved and looked at ended up, after a while, looking at him, just as he ended up looking at them, sometimes fondly, each to the other a special piece of furniture. He let himself settle back into the bed, feeling comfortable and familiar, and he thought,

Nestling, I'm nestling down here—just like everybody else, just before he fell asleep.

• • •

Sometime after noon he went into work. Kelli said Loeffler had called him three times. He was supposed to be working on an incentive plan, but he spent most of the afternoon staring down out his office window at a bench and a pathetic tree set in the sidewalk, wine bottles around the tree reflecting the dirty sunlight. The bench, like all the other damn benches, had "William Donald Schaefer and the Citizens of Baltimore" painted on in script. Blue and white. He thought about calling Paulie at work, but didn't, it became a test of his character, one he passed. When you make love to a woman, he thought, if you accidentally make something, you're supposed to make a son. If you accidentally make a daughter, that's all right, but you're not supposed... It thins out the blood or something. They make this stuff up. He put his feet up on the desk and looked around. Dull, he thought, but not loud, ugly, pathetic, cruel. Decorating an office was like decorating a Buick. He closed his eyes, looking for her, and waited for five o'clock.

When he got to the apartment, she hadn't come home. Tilden fell asleep.

An hour and a half later he woke up on the couch in the living room, in the dark, and reached up where the lamp had been, but then he remembered. So he sat in the dark. He had been having a particularly gaudy dream, he was sweating, but he couldn't remember anything except that it had something to do with work. He never remembered dreams. When he tried, all he could ever bring to mind was the dance dream, which he had had fifteen or more years earlier, a dream about his first wife. Floating around the kitchen of his parents' house in Richmond, she was dancing in the air, in a short, flimsy dress, a 60's dress from Paraphernalia, green with big yellow flowers, and he finally caught her and tied her up with white rope.

Guilt, Tilden thought. People are always talking about guilt, and this is what they mean. I'm feeling guilty, like everybody else. He got up, made his way to the wall switch and stood, thinking about turning it on, decided not to.

On the steps outside the front door, he looked up and his car seemed far away, reflecting a dozen colors from the lights up and down the street. He made himself walk the fifteen feet, took a businesslike look at the traffic on the gray street, circled the brown Toyota, got in. I remember this, Tilden thought, pulling into the traffic. This is high school. He laughed.

When he got to the hotel, he left the car on the street, and was inside before he realized he still didn't know the kid's last name; Tilden stood looking. In the center of the huge, dim lobby, under a high ceiling decorated with lost chandeliers, was a flat fountain where people were pitching pennies into the water. Others sat on gray couches scattered to one side. Tourists were taking photographs of each other around the fountain, using flashes. On the far side of the fountain a recessed bar faced fat green couches set beside stingy glass tables on a gaudy carpet in a slightly darker green. The bar was railed off in brass, and packed. Another recess farther down, and corridors leading off at each corner. The elevator doors, opposite the fountain, were the same smoky marbled mirror glass as the wall. Tilden retreated to the gray couches, sat down, glanced around for short looking men. Boys. Paulie.

Christ, he thought, it's some kind of designer whorehouse. Haven't been in a hotel for ten years. On the other couches, overdressed women, with children standing beside them like miniatures, in crooked coats and ties. He looked around for telephones, but remembered he had no one to call. Hi, thought I'd call to say... well, I'm in love with my daughter... well, I didn't know either... well, she's sort of... tall... no, I'm at her boyfriend's hotel... well, I'm sort of spying on them... only I'm not spying very well... well...

He was cold, and thought of his coat, back at the apartment. He let his head sink into his hands, felt his elbows pressing into his knees, listening to high heels slap across the marble floor. His hair felt greasy. He thought of calling his wife, the second one. Beth. Her name was Beth, and she said she was going to look for somebody who'd let her have a dog. When he tried to picture her, what she looked like, he started to shake. He couldn't hear anything. Then he saw her all in white walking toward him across the lobby, from around the elevators, and, a little behind, a short guy with shaggy hair, black suit, purple shirt, cowboy boots. Paulie, he thought. Paulie, I want to talk to you.

"You don't look well, Tilden," she said, waiting for the boy to arrive beside her. "Ryan, this is my father. Tilden, Ryan."

The boy held out his hand, but then, seeing Tilden's face, withdrew it. "Hello," he said. "Paulinda has told me a great deal about you."

Tilden looked at her. She was shaking her head. This is strange, Tilden thought, he's got to think it's strange. Some quaint American custom, maybe. Perhaps. They say "perhaps."

"I hope you're not angry," Ryan said. "I told Paulie she should call." He looked at her, for an acknowledgement, then at Tilden, and getting nothing, no smile, shook his head. "You are angry. I'm sorry. But this is a little much, you know."

Tilden nodded. "A little much," he said. "Maybe."

Paulie was smiling, carefully. She had the boy's arm, slowly pressing him backward, but he was still talking.

"I am sorry," he said. "And I am pleased to finally meet you." He turned, drew his sleeve from her. "Paulie, I'll see you up—"

Tilden grabbed Ryan's coat, pulled him up onto the balls of his feet; "Little scumbag..." he said. But that was all he could think of. He stared at the kid's face.

He was looking at Tilden as if the older man were a child, a particularly wearisome child, who only had to be outwaited, who couldn't win, but had nonetheless to be allowed some time before the weight of decorum hit him. Tilden let go. "Get rid of him," he said. "He says your name again, I'll kill him."

"You actually do this over here," Ryan said. He was straightening his coat. "I thought it was only in films."

Paulie had stopped smiling. "Tilden, Jesus." She and Ryan exchanged looks, she taking him by the arm and leading him the first few steps back toward the elevators.

When she walked back, she was angry. "Real shabby, daddy. What were you thinking?" She looked around, took Tilden's arm, tightly, and led him toward the broad marble steps down to the street door. "What the hell are you doing here, anyway? You locate some paternal instinct?" She stopped on the steps, cocked her hip, released him, and stared. "Or do you just like making scenes in hotels? You're acting like fifteen."

"I know." Tilden stood three steps down, looking back at her. "But you don't understand."

She laughed, shook her head.

She was wearing some kind of white, long, T-shirt dress,

stretched over her hip in a kind of perfection that only women seemed able to achieve, and it seemed to him that because she fit so perfectly in this hotel lobby, with the Givenchy whorehouse bar, and the orgy of glass and chrome and brass, green and gray and marble and the idiot chandeliers so high no one would call them to come back, and the other people with their impossibly brisk strides and Sunday clothes—what they used to call Sunday clothes—because she fit, so did he. That's how it seemed, but he knew he didn't.

"Call me. Tomorrow," he said. "Tell him I haven't been well or something. Call me at work."

He smiled and turned his face away, didn't look back until he was through the glass doors and out on the sidewalk. She was posed on the broad marble steps. He stood on the sidewalk, staring back over something written in gold on the glass, her clear eyes, the black hair, soft breasts with the big nipples, her hip high, and he felt his eyes smile and felt them blink once, twice, three, four times, and he thought, You can't look at anyone this way unless you've slept with her, and she, smiling, stepped back up a step. He jerked forward, a fraction of an inch, looked down, then back up at her for another second's worth of it, then raised his hand and waved. Someone was standing behind him, a copy of the *Sun* under her arm, looking at him like he was some sort of space creature. Tilden smiled. He wanted to look back through the glass doors. The woman circled around him and into the hotel.

• • •

The next day, a Tuesday, she never called, but around three

thirty Tilden was looking out his window when they came up the street and stopped at the corner. A short boy and a tall girl, arguing. They worked their way toward the building and then worked their way away. She was coming; he was going. When the boy began winning the argument, they would fade toward the sad little tree and the bench for the bus. When she got the upper hand, toward the building they came. Her dress was light, nylon or polyester, and swung as the boy grabbed her arm and released it, grabbed again. She threw her hands up, threw her head back, sat down on the bench. Tilden's telephone buzzed.

"Yes," he said, and then, "Okay," and then, "Oh, Kelli, when Paulie... If Paulie comes, just send her in," and then Tiny Loeffler came on the line.

"Let me guess," Loeffler said. "You've been busy—that teenager you had up here last month? You recall we talked about an incentive plan? We're tired of hiring new tellers every week. So think of something. You know, nifty prizes."

"We could pay them a living wage," Tilden said. He was straightening the telephone cord. "Microwaves again?"

"That's a breaththrough," Loeffler said.

Tilden snorted. "If they aren't going to okay cash, the whole thing is a waste anyway. I can do you up a microwave plan by five this afternoon, no problem." The telephone cord was stretched out flat. They were still on the bench. Her arms were down, one hand caressing the hem of the dress, her black hair sparkling in the sunlight.

"Okay, but hurry the hell up."

His left hand, with the receiver, fell to his side; he could hear Loeffler talking, distantly. "Put your arms around her," Tilden said, "you sleazy little creep." He laughed and pulled the phone back up.

"You there? Tilden? Hey, what's that little girl's name? She in the book?"

Tilden was silent, turned away from the window. He felt blank, holding the telephone, waiting.

"Okay," Loeffler said, "but I think she needs a younger man. You're a little long in the tooth here. Aren't you? Has her daddy seen you yet? Hey?"

Tilden began to smile. "I'm her daddy," he said. "Her name is Paulinda. She's my daughter. You ought to get married, Tiny."

He heard part of a laugh, then silence, then a click, and the dial tone. Tilden, listening, stepped back to the window. She was straightening herself, patting her hair, setting seams, shifting her shoulders. Cotton. The dress was cotton. He set the telephone receiver down. I'm not a bad guy, Tilden thought, for wanting this woman to be wearing a nylon dress, for wanting to look at her, for wanting her to hush and put her hands on me, for any of it. She'll be quiet now, and go away. She's already gone. Maybe sometime she'll need money, and she'll call. He looked around the room. Place's okay, he thought. Peaceful. You ought to have a kid.

He stood at the tall blue windows which stretched to the floor—it made you sick when you stood close—and looked to his right then back to his left, but the street was empty. In his mind he saw them again, moving, talking, a mimed argument on the blue and white bench. Stand up, sit down. Stand up, sit down. I remember that, he thought. He reached out, his hand moving as if by itself, and touched the thick glass.

Jealous You, Jealous Me

Okay so it wasn't *really* four women, but by the end of it the two of them felt like two women each. Busy over here, busy over there, back over here, and so on. You just let one look go wrong, or say something, or one smirking over finishing a goddamn crossword first, or even one of them too quick and loud shouting out an answer ("Ort!") and Bam! there goes your ménage à trois. Go back to Catholic school.

But in the beginning it was fun, and the porno part was just part of it, and not even the best part. Life got much bigger, for all three of us. They were surprised, I think, how interested they were in each other, that they liked each other. It was walking down streets in the snow, travelling in threes, kidding, cooking, staring, or showing up together at parties, stepping around in some over-hardwooded apartment, and watching everyone we knew wonder, their blasé eyes a little too open. Guessing. And then, on the way back to one of our own apartments, running and laughing, rolling around in the snowbank on the side of the hill that fell away down from the street. Kids.

It was electric, watching them shopping at a secondhand shop together, or coming in the door back from the market on the other side of the park with leaves on their clothes, in their glorious hair. Or standing on the sidewalk by myself one early evening, big coat and cold, looking up toward the building, finding our window, watching shadows move in the apartment, wondering myself, crazy with sweet slow blood-pounding jealousy.

In Catholic school the electricity of sin was everywhere possible, in a word, a wish, a thought, making the simplest action—a look—a cataclysm, a murder. What wasn't itself a sin was an "occasion of sin." What a way to live. I loved it. But later when you lost faith in sins, there was this catastrophic collateral cost. Now, with the two of them, things mattered again in that old way I had all but forgotten. I got it all back for a while.

Our park was mostly an overgrown field stretched between rocks high on one side and a creek in a ravine shrouded by trees on the other. Once, in the spring, in the middle of the field I turned over a two foot square piece of weathered plywood and found a small Storeria, Dekay's Snake, about ten inches long, and picked it up. I knew from when I was a kid. She was on one side of me in jeans, and she was on the other side in jeans, and because wonders were welcome, this parlor skill I had picked up as a loner ten year old was thrilling, magical, like jumping motorcycles or something. Suddenly come running up two scrawny boys about ten, the lead one yelling, "That's my snake, *mister!*" I looked at him. He was pointing at the muddy plywood. "It's my snake… trap," he said, still fierce, and took the Dekay's when I offered it. It was his snake trap. That was what the spring was like, perfect things happened.

So why, what happened later? We moved. We got jobs in another city and all moved there, and everything seemed to go out of balance. If you have ever been in a bed with two women made wholly and entirely of concrete, you can imagine the experience. Otherwise, no.

No, the real reason was that I left it up to them. Maybe there was no alternative. Maybe one of them had been waiting all along to undo it, I don't know. Diffidence was perfect for creating balance in the beginning and while things were going well. I never tried to control things, to say this and not that. I said only I want you and I want you, which in our electrified air, seemed to be enough.

I might've saved it if I had tried. Might not.

But now I wish just for a few minutes, or an hour, or days, or the rest of a life of that jealousy, the feeling outside on the sidewalk, in the instant lost and alone in the most acute way, looking up waiting to see through a window a shadow move against a wall, knowing but also imagining where the couch and chair and kitchen and bed were in the apartment, wondering if they were touching each other, with the key in my pocket.

Down the Garden Path

At the airport Danny was wearing a suit and tie, and I almost didn't recognize him. He had cut the hair and the hostile little beard he had worn ever since I had known him, since I met and married his mother.

"Hey, Thomas," he said, when he turned and found me looking uncertainly at him, frowning, standing just outside the screening area. He stuck out his hand and I shook it and threw my arm around his shoulder, stiffly. Danny looked like his father, square-jawed, clean shaven, with that noncommittal smile which was all in his eyes. His father had been a hero, of a sort of obvious sort.

Without all the extra hair he seemed somehow less formidable, wide-eyed, a little childish, innocent, even though he was twenty-six, even though eight years earlier he had killed another boy with his hands in a fight and whenever I was around him that was what I thought of, no matter what he looked like. It was impossible not to see it when I looked at him. They had both been deep into drugs, but the other kid had attacked him and it happened out of state and the circumstances were muddy in other ways. After thirty thousand dollars in lawyers, finally he was no-billed. I remember the lawyers charged us four thousand dollars for Xeroxing. None of it seemed to chasten or change him much, but Laura never really recovered.

He had been in college when she and I married, and my

acquaintance with him which was always strained was also always only a passing one, so it didn't much matter. After college he played music, went to live in Hawaii, then California, and later in Tucson, and periodically we would send him money. Now, Laura was dead, and he had come home to bury her.

We were standing out on the main concourse and Danny was talking but I was disoriented, having trouble paying attention. On the drive to the airport, alone, and later trying to walk away the time until the plane got in, I had been talking to myself, not quite making sense. The place felt odd, otherworldly. I hadn't been to the airport in years. I was not in good shape, but it would be better now with someone to talk to, even if it was Danny.

I had been, for several years, involved with a woman, a friend of ours named Marianne, and she had been helping me take care of Laura, as much as we could care for her at the hospital. In the last month or so I had become completely dependent on Marianne for my psychological balance. Left alone, in an hour or so I would start to come unraveled. But having now another person to deal with forced me to regain some composure, a sort of cure by etiquette.

Danny curled a magazine in his hands like it was a baseball bat, looked quickly up and down the blue-carpeted concourse, and said, "You want to wait up here?"

I shook my head and we started toward the escalators. The terminal was oddly empty on the upper floor. He walked fast, as if we could do something about his mother if we could only get there in time. We rode down to the lower floor to pick up his bag. Downstairs, there were a lot more people.

"So, how are you doing?" Danny said, while we were waiting next to the empty conveyor belt. He was leaning against a big two-foot square white column, ill at ease, not used to wearing a suit coat. It was an expensive coat, but ill-fitting and more rumpled than an airplane flight was likely to cause. The tie, red and yellow and so short it seemed like a gag gift, made me oddly angry.

"I'm okay," I said. "A little weird, maybe. You all right?"

He pushed away from the square column, a stage pause to give me this theatrical, questioning look. "My mother is dead."

I sighed. I stood with my arms crossed, staring, trying to remember what twenty-six was like, trying to think of anything we had in common, beside loving the same dead woman. Trying not to hate him. I looked around at the other people, a lot of them dressed up, good-looking women, men with money, old people. They looked intensely healthy. The difference, I thought, is that I've already asked all these questions and now he has to ask them. We're out of phase, is all. "Danny, they tried everything they could," I said. "I told you on the—"

"You told me they said—"

"She's dead, Danny. I'm sorry. Everything I told you was stuff they told me, and none of it ever quite scanned. The last four days she was in a coma. Only they wouldn't call it a coma. They—"

I looked at him, then walked away, past a fat guy in a uniform checking baggage tags, and over to a bench by the front windows where I sat down. I had told him what they told me on Monday which was that she had one chance in ten, and that chance was for another month or two. That was Monday. The Friday before, surgery was impossible but a special chemotherapy might arrest it, and the Friday before that it was an "aggressive approach" combining surgery with chemotherapy, as soon as they got the calcium down, might buy as much as a year. They had gotten the calcium down, and she'd stopped hallucinating. On the third Friday she died. They talk all this talk with you, like they're letting you in, like it's shoptalk, and you forget that you don't know what they're talking about and that they're just guessing, that they don't know what they're talking about.

Danny walked up with his suitcase. "Let's get out of here."

I stood up, and pointed toward a sort of hallway. "It's that way." We started on our way to the parking. The hallway narrowed and then opened into a long space with a series of glass doors to the outside. The doors were framed in brass which looked hammered or patterned like the doors to an old downtown hotel. This was weird, because the rest of the airport looked like it had a thin coat of sci-fi movie. "You'll stay at the house, won't you?" I said, as I followed him out.

"Yeah, okay," Danny said.

By the time we got onto the freeway into the city it was just after dark, the lights from strip centers on either side of the six-lane road creating a false twilight. Lightning flashed along the horizon, a distant thunderstorm. Danny was quiet. He punched the car radio on, then punched it off. I thought about driving back and forth to the hospital, the last few weeks, two or three times a day. They wouldn't say she was in a "coma," just "unconscious"; there was some difference.

Then one day last week the doctor I liked, Thompson, a heavyset, gently graying, quiet guy took me down a hall, up a floor, and into some odd room that seemed to be directly behind a nurses' station. There were shelves and a lot of white stuff, packaging, it was some kind of supply room. He said they had now done everything they could. I was in a chair; he was half-sitting against a table or a desk. When he said she was "comfortable," I started shaking and shouting, "She's fucking comatose, how the fuck do you know?" but he just stood watching me, until I felt stupid. I apologized.

Danny watched the city pass by outside the car window. He wouldn't look at me. He was blaming me for letting his mother die. I shook my head, to lose the thought.

He was a nice-looking kid, six one, dark brows, with brown eyes set wide apart and an odd un-aimed stare that used to be a mannerism of movie stars, a vulnerable or stunned look. Montgomery Clift, James Dean. The look was surly, too, sometimes. When I first knew him, the anger he broadcast unsettled me, but now it annoyed me more than anything else. Yeah, I'm angry, too, I thought.

I had worked with Laura for some years before her divorce and a couple years after it we started seeing each other. When I met Danny he was already fifteen, already a petty criminal. With her gone, I felt no obligation to pretend to like him.

We had never gotten along very well, anyway, but I thought we could go through the motions of this and get it done. It was only two days, the official part. When someone you love dies, your father, your mother, it's not something that happens on one particular day so much as something that settles in, over a long time, so two years later you're still talking to her, in your head, and the sadness kind of grows over her absence.

"Is there any money?" Danny said, finally, after we were off the freeway, and I had turned onto the street the house was on.

"Can we bury her first?" I said, then lifted my hands away from the steering wheel. "Sorry. I didn't mean that. I was thinking about something else."

He frowned. "I just meant, what happens? She had a rent house, in Austin, and some other stuff, government bonds or something, from grandpa, before she married you. My dad didn't leave her anything. I just wondered what happens to it."

"She left it all to me, Danny." When I saw his shocked look in the light from the streetlights, I said, "I'm supposed to look out for you, that was the idea. It's your money. It amounts to about seventy thousand dollars." I turned into the driveway, pulled the car up to the garage doors, and shut it off. "But we can talk about it. Later. I'll write you a check or something, after the legalities are settled. And after your lecture, after I speak sternly to you about husbandry."

He frowned. "I thought husbandry was farming," he said, shrugged, and leaned back in the seat. "I'm twenty-seven," he said.

"No," I said. "You're not." He's just a kid, I thought, and his mother just died. His father had died when Danny was about eleven. His father, the legend, the hell-raiser with the big Harley and the big dogs, malamutes, who in all his photographs looks like he's lying. Killed himself on the motorcycle, about a year after their divorce.

We got out of the car and walked in through the kitchen door. I had no reason to dislike him, really, other than that he disliked me.

"I want some things," he said, setting his suitcase down and looking around the kitchen. He wandered over to the table and pulled out one of the chairs and sat down. "Sentimental things. We can talk about it later," he said.

"Okay."

"It's stuff we used to have," he said, "when we lived on Weston, in that little apartment. And there's some jewelry, too. She had this necklace she used to let me play with, when I was a kid. It was sapphires, for God's sake, and she used to let me play with it. My dad probably stole it, burglary or something." He looked at me. "It was beautiful."

"I know the necklace," I said, and walked over to the

refrigerator, swung it open. "You want a beer? You can't have it."

He was staring at me and he was sort of smiling, as if he thought we were in a contest and he was winning. The smile probably worked real well for him in bars or wherever he hung out.

"You want a beer? Orange juice? Diet Pepsi?" I reached in and took a bottle of beer. When I tried to twist off the top, it tore my hand, so I shuffled around in a drawer until I found an opener.

"You have any liquor?"

I pointed to a cabinet below the counter. He got up to get himself a drink and I carried my beer over to the table and sat down. "Where'd you get that fancy coat?"

"Goodwill," Danny said, adding water from the tap to his glass. "Can I get it pressed tomorrow? On Sunday?" He got some ice from the freezer and stirred with his fingers. "What is this stuff, bourbon? Maybe I could press it myself," he said. "We got an iron?"

"You could wear one of mine, maybe."

"This'll do," Danny said. "Mom won't care. You could loan me a tie. She probably won't recognize me, wherever she is." He took a big drink from his glass and grimaced. "Nasty," he said. "Sheez. Think I'll take a beer after all. He looked at the liquor in his glass, glanced at me, and then poured it into the sink.

I stood up. "I've got a couple telephone calls. Could you put some beer in the freezer? There're only four or five cold ones. Put a whole six-pack up there. There's food, some ham and some leftover Popeye's chicken. Carrots and applesauce. Your room is at the end of the hall." He looked at me. "Right," I said. "You know where the room is. I'll be upstairs."

"Okay," Danny said.

As I started away, the front doorbell rang, and Danny looked at me in a peculiar sort of way. Maybe I just imagined it. It would be Marianne at the door, and introducing her to Danny made me paranoid. Marianne was already angry, and there was a lot I didn't want to explain to Danny. Marianne had been my lover for about two years, and even been Laura's lover for a few months at the beginning. She'd spent every day with me most of the last two weeks. She had wanted to come to the airport with me and gotten angry and walked out when I insisted not.

I headed for the door through the dim living room, lit only by a small lamp at a desk against the far wall. Just something else to do, to get through. Something else to postpone sadness for. This is why some people sob and scream, have their grief on time and at the top of their lungs. But the truth was that I was glad she was there. Being with Danny was too close to being alone.

"Is it okay?" she said, when I opened the door.

I nodded, leaned forward to kiss her long dark hair, and then stepped out of the way. "I'm glad you came," I said. We stood in the entryway. And then I laughed. "He's not going to understand," I said. "He's a little simple."

"That'll be unpleasant," she said. "But it's not a big thing."

"It feels bad. Hating him."

Danny came to the door at the other end of the living room and stood looking at us with a new beer in his hand. He can't have finished that that quickly, I thought. I felt, of course, caught, like he was the girl's father, but I put my hand to Marianne's back and we started over to him.

"Marianne," I said, "this is my stepson, Danny. Danny, Marianne."

"Hello," Danny said, blankly, and he shook her hand.

"I'm so sorry about your mother," Marianne said. "She was about my best friend in the world." She looked at me.

"Marianne took care of us the last seven months," I said. "Let's go in the kitchen."

"No, I think I want to stay in here," Danny said and he let his body fall onto one of the couches.

I had started for the kitchen. "Suit yourself," I said. He was staring at Marianne in the dim light, and when I looked at her I saw her again as if for the first time, beautiful hair, long sad face, shining eyes.

"No," she said, "let's sit in here." And she settled in the armchair between the two couches.

"Whatever," I said. "Do you want something?" I waved toward the kitchen. "I have a beer."

She shook her head. I went into the kitchen and threw ice in a glass and poured the rest of my beer into it, got another from the refrigerator. They didn't speak. I walked back in and sat on a couch opposite my stepson, set the glass and the beer on the low table.

"Danny's been living in Arizona," I said. "Did you ever put out that EP or whatever it was, Danny?"

"Smells like pussy in here," he said, looking at me with that empty stare of his.

"Okay, you little motherfucker," I said, "I'm not—"

"That would be me," Marianne said. She hadn't moved, but there was the slightest smile on her lips. "And your point is?"

"My point is that you guys were screwing your way to bliss while my mother—and his wife—was dying and puking her guts out in a hospital by herself. And now you sit in her house like you own the place. You fuck on that couch?"

She laughed. "So you're like the Holy Ghost?" she said. "This is a great country where the utterly ignorant get to have opinions on everything, and usually do. Actually, Laura was almost never alone because he was there, pretty much all the time, and so was I. 'Please go home, both of you. Eat a hot fudge sundae for me.' I don't recall seeing you. Did you hear me tell you she was the best friend I ever had?"

"Sure. Yeah, I heard that." He smirked.

Marianne sat forward in the armchair. "Do you know what a friend is?"

"No, no, no, no," I said. "That's enough of this." When he started to say something, I held my hand up, shook my head. "No, don't. You can think anything you want, but you've said enough. I'm sorry that you've lost your mama, that must be terrible. I have a sense of how that is." I took out my wallet, took out a credit card. "Here, go get your bag, get yourself a motel room, call a cab."

He stood up, looked at me. "It's my house," he said, feebly.

"You know that's not so," I said. "You've got your grief, that's all you've got. I've got mine." I shook my head again. "And I don't want your dirt on it, no matter how bad you feel. So go on."

When he was gone, we sat in the living room for a while. I wanted a cigarette, even though I had quit smoking fifteen years before. It was ten minutes before either one of us said anything.

"I'm sorry," Marianne said. "You were right, though. You can't share grief."

"Nothing to be sorry about." I smiled at her. "You know,

the funny thing is that when he was trying to be so ugly, I felt
horribly sad for him. It was the first time all day I didn't just
hate his guts. I'm sorry you had to listen to it, though. Poor
little fuck."

She shrugged, kicked her fingers through her hair, settled
back into the chair. It reminded me of Laura a little bit. I remembered once a long time ago, lying around with her on
another Sunday, and I must have been reading the classifieds
because for some reason I was reading her a Lost and Found
ad for a dog which said something like "German Shepherd, 19
months, standard black and tan, choke collar, XQ181714 tat-
tooed inside right ear..." and it went on like that for a while,
and Laura laughed and said, "That dog's not lost. That dog just
left." Not the sort of thing you remember about your beloved
after they die, but there it is. And I thought, the kid didn't get
that stunned look from the movies, and he didn't get it from
his father. That was her look. He got it from her.

Tahiti

Lucas looked up, squinting into the black guts of the MG, watching his fingers guide a bolt into place. "You're pretty," he said. "Pretty—But dumb." He reached back over his shoulder, turned his head to the side, caught the sweat on his forehead with the sleeve of his T-shirt. "You know how much time I spent looking for you last night? Half hour. You may just be the dumbest bolt on this whole goddamn car, you know that? That's right, that's a sweet child, just one second now, that's right—" He reached back again, his fingers a spider across the concrete, closing around a socket, bringing it back and pushing it onto the ratchet, one-handed, his other hand on the bolt up beside the timing chain cover. He reached up with the ratchet. "One more second, and you're home. Tick, tick, tickety, tick. Tick. There. You know, I knew a bolt on a combine once that was just almost as dumb as you are. A farm bolt. You're dumber than a farm bolt." He let his shoulders settle on the concrete, took a long, slow breath, stretched his neck out.

Lucas slid out from under the MG, wiped his hands on a red rag, walked into the house and stopped in the kitchen. He looked through the doorway into the rest of the house. "Liz?" he yelled, and waited. No answer. She wasn't back from the school.

He picked four white window envelopes off the green kitchen table, shuffled through them, and set them back down, leaving shadowy fingerprints. Bills. He liked the way they felt, fat with extras, sharp with creases. The MG would be worth five or six hundred, after the parts and the machine shop. And the VW brake job was worth another hundred. Two damn Fiats supposed to come in, a clutch job and a tune-up. And Liz would get eight or so from the college, at the end of the month.

And it's only the sixteenth, he thought. So we're flush. "Flush." Jesus, Daddy's word. You want to live without money? Go to Tahiti. He meant it, too, all that time he was hoping I would really go; would have been almost like going himself. Figuring that out only took me ten years. The genius.

He checked the clock on the microwave on the counter. 5:04. She should've been here an hour ago, he thought. His hand hurt. He looked at it, flexed the fingers, rubbed it with his other hand. Then he went back out to the garage and the MG.

An hour later, when Liz pulled up and got out of her little station wagon, he stopped to watch her walk the driveway. She was beautiful, in a white blouse with wide sleeves, skirt above the knee, black hose. Her sparkling hair pulled back—the only compromise with college etiquette. Lucas had been, as always, asleep when she left in the morning.

"Jesus," he said, and smiled. "University lets teachers dress like that nowadays? You're trying to break some poor kid's heart or something?"

She stopped in front of him, beside the little white car, kicked her knee up a little, drew her shoulders back. "Oh, I already did." She reached up to loosen her hair.

"The genius? He's made for getting his heart broke. Little snot."

"How do you know he's a little snot?" she said. "You've never even met him."

Lucas shrugged. "Professor, what you describe is a little

snot. I know it through the acuity of..." He turned to see what she was looking at, but it was only the car. "Maybe it's some faculty heart you're trying to break."

She laughed, gave him a look.

"Right," he said. "Those parties. The chin-less hordes."

"Join me in a little leftover whatever?" She pointed to the kitchen door. "Spaghetti? It was good spaghetti, wasn't it? You about finished here?"

"It's all back together," he said. "I was just setting the valves. Manifolds, carbs, and tune it, and I get—"

"Get paid." She ran her finger along the top of the white fender, leaned back to look at the MG. "I always liked these little cars. Do you think the woman'll sell it?"

Lucas looked at her, blinked. "I know he's a little snot because I used to be a genius. And I was a little snot."

"What's it worth?" she said, still looking at the car.

He shook his head. "Now? With the new engine? About two grand. Twenty-five hundred, if she's lucky."

"Oh," she said, and smiled, and walked into the house.

They ate dinner and made love, and watched television and drank beer, and made love again, and she fell asleep after, nude in the big bed she always complained about, because it was like a rock, a thin mattress on a sheet of oversized plywood, really, not a bed, something else on the list of things to buy. Like insurance. He stood at the window, listening to the cool air push through the air conditioner register in the ceiling.

At the bare window, smoking, he looked out at the street and his neighbors' houses, most of which had gone dark by now, until a couple cars turned the corner, washing him with their headlights, from the waist up. There was light from the streetlight, too, so he took her dark brown silk robe from a peg by the bathroom door and slipped it on. Kimono. It was delicate, soft, smelled like her hair. He felt like some forties movie star or something.

But he didn't want to stand at the window anymore. What he really wanted was to make love again, the way they used to, so that it lasted forty-five minutes, and in the midst of it you didn't know where you were. Need a new one for that, he thought. New ones are so much trouble. He sat in the director's chair next to the bed in the dim light and watched her sleep, remembering ten years earlier, the not thinking.

Like insurance. He could have mentioned insurance, Lucas thought, while he was going on and on about Pacific islands and money. But he probably did. Insurance, boy, that's how you know you're old, you find yourself craving insurance. That, and that first time when you get down to look under a car, or a couch, play with the baby, pick up something you dropped, whatever... and you think: Jesus, that hurts. That didn't used to hurt. If we had a kid, then thirty-six years later he could stand at some window somewhere and think about all the things I told him wrong, or didn't tell him. He stood up.

She moved, sighed in her sleep, stretched and turned in the bed, and came to rest on her back, with one knee pulled up. Her face looked like a child's face, very serious. He sat down on the bed and reached across to touch her, drew his hand down along her side to her hard hip bone standing high just below her waist, and leaned over to kiss her. She smiled in her sleep. I could do this every night, he thought. But we don't. He pulled his legs up on the hard mattress and settled his head back. The silk hissed as he straightened the robe. Turn the thermostat up, he thought. Tomorrow, she'll be home all day; she can sit out in the shop with me while I do the carburetors. Go out to dinner. He reached out with his hand, let it rest on her thigh, and fell asleep.

In the morning she slept late, and he laughed when he discovered the brown robe tight on his arms and wound around his legs. He dressed, drank some coffee and left to pick up rebuild kits for the MG's old carburetors.

The parts place was a big tin shed, glassed across the front, but it took direct afternoon sun and the glass had been tinted. Inside, it smelled like grease. Callie, the boy at the counter, said, "Put some SUs on there, Luke. Get that sad old bus up on its hind legs."

Lucas just looked at him. "It's an MG," he said. "Doesn't matter what kind of carbs you put on it."

"Yeah, guess not," Callie said, flipping through one of the big specifications books on top of the counter. He drew his finger across one of the pages, mumbled numbers to himself. "You could bore it out. With a couple sticks of dynamite."

Lucas laughed. "I could weld a Testarossa to the rear bumper," he said, "but I ain't gonna. How about just giving me the Stromberg kits."

The kid twirled around and disappeared back into the tall gray metal shelving overstuffed with one-color printed boxes and plastic packages and cardboard with crude Marks-a-Lot notations and numbers.

Callie always wanted everything to go faster than it possibly could, wanted to blow the transmission out of every car he got his hands on, and, often, he succeeded. Lucas remembered being like that once. And country roads. Now he just liked the hardware, the bolts and brackets and washers and sleeves, the way the case hardened steel looked new, the perfect black rubber O-rings, the way it all spoke to you when it worked,

187

quietly, the way years later, and in another country, you sat around sometimes figuring backwards what some engineer in England, or Germany, or Italy, or Japan, had figured frontwards years before. Like talking to somebody you never could know, Lucas thought, really talking to him, about something you both loved. But it started with the hardware. He picked up one of the little boxes from the counter where Callie had set them.

"You want new needles? Jets? Floats?"

Lucas shook his head. "The old ones are okay." He emptied the box out into his hand, looking at the O-rings, gaskets, a shining aluminum washer. "Nice stuff, isn't it?" he said, holding his open hand out.

Callie drummed his fingers on the counter. "Duh," he said, and smirked.

Lucas looked up.

"You want the brake stuff, too?" Callie said. "What year's the VW?"

• • •

When he got home, Liz's car was still there. She's probably still asleep, he thought, until the kitchen door lock clicked as he got into the garage. He put the carburetor kits on the shelf running along the outside kitchen wall.

"Have you eaten anything?" he heard her say. He smelled bacon, before he drew the screen open and stepped inside. "People are supposed to eat," she said. "I mean, before they get to where they're about to pass out. You can do the eggs. I always break them."

He put his arm around her lightly, kissed the side of her face, through her hair.

"You go to Eurasian? You were gone a long time."

He nodded, walked to the hall doorway, stood watching her turn the bacon in the old heavy black frying pan.

"What are you looking at?"

He slid his hands into his pockets. "Let's go out to dinner. Tonight, I mean."

She stopped, fork above frying pan, and turned halfway around. "We have a guest for dinner." She set the fork on the stove beside the pan, reached up to open a cabinet. "Tonight."

"Who?" he said. "Why didn't you…"

"I asked Gordon Greer if he'd like to come to dinner."

"Oh, Jesus, Liz." He was shaking his head. "You're kidding? What are you, his mother all of a sudden? We're adopting him? Why the hell didn't you tell me?"

"He's a very special kid. And he's a thousand miles from home." She took two plates out of the cabinet, shut it, and set the plates side by side on the counter.

"You aren't paid to be a nanny. You have to feed the kids too? C'mon. We'll have to buy a silver spoon for the twit."

"Luke—"

"They treat you like garbage over there. They've got guys who spend whole days looking for their chins and they pay them eight times what they pay you. Adjunct. Emphasis on 'junct.'"

"That has nothing to—"

"They teach a course the first semester and spend the second semester deciding how many sheets each professor gets from the Xerox machine. Duh. You don't get any."

She reached out and flipped the gas off, picked up the fork. The flame under the frying pan flared yellow and went out. "That has nothing to do with Gordon Greer. He needs attention."

"Jesus. *I* need attention. I mean, okay, he's special, he's a genius. Great. Maybe he'll do right and get his MBA and screw his teacher in his spare time."

She threw the fork and it bounced up out of the pan and over the edge of the stove and fell to the floor. "You could've finished. You could still finish. But you like to screw with cars. Like, like—"

"Yeah?" he said. "Like?"

"Well, like your old man. And his goddamn farm. Maybe if somebody had taken an interest, you wouldn't have flunked out."

He watched her walk across the kitchen, sit at the table. "I didn't flunk out," he said, following her. "I quit. And I wasn't eighteen, I was in graduate school. And, for that matter, lots of them took an interest, whatever that means. I was a freak, they always 'take an interest' in freaks."

"Well…" she said. She stared up at him. "I told him about you. That you were happy. That school was just school. I told him he didn't have to be a genius. Only I didn't say 'genius.' I told him he could go to Tahiti, live on the beach. Or work on cars if he wanted to." She looked away.

"So I'm sort of an exhibit or something?"

"Everything I told him was stuff you told me." She wouldn't look at him. She was crying.

"Okay, okay, we'll have a nice dinner. I'll wear overalls. No, I'll wear a tux, and we can smear gear oil on it. The happy prole. Elizabeth? Jesus, if you'll stop crying I'll go to work for GT&E. Procter and Gamble. Anybody, I don't care…"

"I don't want you to go to work for anybody."

"Yeah, I know. Look, I just wanted to go to dinner. Just

you and me. Alone." He sat on the edge of the table, stood back up, stepped toward the door. "Fine, okay, we'll have dinner. Stop crying. Jesus. I'm going to work."

He walked out, stood listening until he heard the pan clanking on the stove again, and sat down at the bench, picked up a carburetor, and thought about his breakfast. She'd bring it out, she wouldn't break the eggs, but she'd overcook them, they'd be solid, but when you're hungry, who cares? He thought of his mother, standing out on the porch, what the farm did to her, always tired, and angry, and it was because they didn't have any money, and that was why his father never talked about anything else, wanted him to run off to a desert island, and make a million there.

• • •

The kid arrived at seven. He was big and, except for his light, klutzy hair, rugged looking, not at all what Lucas had guessed. Liz led the way through the living room, and they settled at the kitchen table.

"I hate my name," the kid said, after Liz had introduced them. "I sound like some movie star everybody forgot about."

"Gloria Graham."

"Lucas," Liz said, but the kid laughed and nodded at him across the table.

He and Liz had found the table at a Goodwill store—an old green-marble formica dinette table with an aluminum band around the edge. He had gotten the bumper shop to re-chrome the legs. It looked brand new, resurrected, but the kid treated it like it was just some dumb table.

"You even know who Gloria Graham was?"

"Lucas!" she said again.

"Well," Gordon said, "I saw her in a movie, with Robert Mitchum. He's a doctor. She owns these horses, a stallion and a mare. When she finally goes to bed with Robert Mitchum, the horses go berserk." He giggled. "It was funny. It was a real fifties movie."

"Well, shut my mouth," Lucas said.

Liz laughed.

The kid was leaning forward, broad-shouldered and big arms, looking like he played on the line. A tackle or something. What must it be like to be a tackle, Lucas thought. Go around saying, I'm a tackle. I'm a mechanic. I'm a genius. The names they give us to call ourselves.

"Gordon watches a lot of movies," Liz said.

"I hear you're a genius, Gordon."

The kid looked at Liz, back at Lucas.

"I've got to get the vegetables cut up." Liz pushed her chair back from the table. "You all will excuse me? Gordon's thinking about quitting school, Luke. Maybe you can help him with that." She pointed toward the hall door. "In the living room."

The kid started to say something, but Lucas said, looking at Liz, "We can help you."

She pointed again. "Help most by staying out of the way." She stared at him, held the look an extra second, then went for the refrigerator. "It's Thai chicken. Sometimes this comes out, sometimes it doesn't. When it comes out, it's terrific."

"You watch TV, Gordon?" Lucas said, taking his glass from the green table. "You want to watch TV?" He walked into the hall, turned into the living room.

The kid followed, close behind. "I—I usually watch

movies. Do you have Showtime? There're some great movies on Showtime. And HBO and Cinemax," he said. "They're pay channels."

Lucas looked at him, pointed to the couch, sat in his chair. "Yeah, I know. But my trust fund was late this month."

The kid shrugged, smiled with his eyes, a six-year-old. He sat forward on the couch, stiff, like a museum exhibit.

Genius, Lucas thought. Should have a brass plaque. "You know the first time I heard someone say, 'I only watch movies'?" he said, rubbing his hand, looking at it. He glanced at Gordon. "It was a while back. It's okay to do it, just don't say it."

The kid put his hands on the couch, lifted himself, settled in the identical position at the front edge. "You—You're a car mechanic? But you used to be a psychologist," he said. "I thought about trying to be a psychologist. Must be strange. I mean, being both. I mean, you must have been smart."

"I was in school," Lucas said. "Seems like forever. I was never a psychologist."

"Did she really say that, about me?" the kid said. When he said 'she,' he held the word in the air as long as he could.

Lucas laughed. "Yeah, I'm afraid so." He picked up the remote control and punched the TV on, no sound. The picture flashed and then came in. A living room, unbearably sterile. Some pale black people talking. Lucas looked around his own living room, at the secondhand furniture, and the tables and couch he'd built and she'd sewn. Number 2 yellow pine modern, her snotty colleague had called it. But he wasn't being snotty. Liked it better than I do, Lucas thought. Wished he had built it himself.

"It's a great view," the kid said. He was looking out the big front window, at the streetlights and the streets sloping down away from the house. "I like to just watch cars drive up and down. Wonder what they're thinking, the drivers. I imagine them going to meet somebody." He laughed, a short little laugh. "There's this cop in the McDonald's every Friday night. His cop car is always outside. He's always sitting with this nervous looking woman. She's beautiful, but she's nervous. They're in love, I think. It's great. She has her hair up, like..." He put his hand to the back of his head. "Her hair is beautiful, too, just pulled up tight. They're always in the corner, at a corner table. Hiding. It's great." As he looked at Lucas, the wild smile began to fade from his face. "You and Miss—"

"Liz. You can call her Liz."

"You and... Liz... are like that," the kid said. "She talks about you." He looked away. As the energy slipped out of him, his wide soft face looked empty, dead. A big, dead kid, a shape.

Lucas closed his eyes, hearing his breathing. Kitchen, he thought, and got up from the chair, then picked up his glass, pointed at Gordon's. "Hey. You want something? A beer?" He was staring at the quiet boy. "Anything?"

The kid shook his head.

• • •

In the kitchen, Liz was standing at the sink. "I'm a jerk," Lucas said, "a proletarian ex-genius jerk. I thought I was over it. But I've—" She was holding one hand wrapped around the other. She was white. The counter stretched off under a mess of paper towels, plastic bags, cut up tomatoes and peppers and onions. Ginger root cut like pale gold poker chips. The big knife, with blood on it.

"I'm all right," she said. Tears in her eyes. "Only I only don't feel very well."

"Let me see it."

The sink was full of blood. Her index finger was dark, with a crescent-shaped cut curving in a black line at the side of the tip. He put his arm around her shoulders. "Emergency clinic," he said. "Okay?"

"No," she said. "No. I'm not spending forty-six dollars on a stupid little cut."

"Is it throbbing?" He drew his arm away, put it back.

"You cut yourself worse than this all the time. I feel so stupid. I want to sit down."

He led her to the table, lowered her onto one of the chairs. "Did you wash it? Put some—Some—"

She nodded. "It was like a big fat flap on the end of my finger. But I put some pressure on it and it went right back."

"It'll be all right," Lucas said. "It'll be okay."

"I wasn't looking what I was doing."

"It'll be okay. You just sit there." He walked back to the refrigerator, reached in for a beer, and set it beside the cut vegetables on the counter. He looked back at her, opened a cabinet, took out a glass, and took the glass and the beer over to the table and poured for her. "You drink. We'll cook," he said. "Gordon!" he shouted. "Need you in here." She looked sheepish, drying her eyes before the kid got into the kitchen.

He arrived all smiles, lumbering through the hall doorway and over between them, his light hair soft and babyish, his bulk not quite under control, until he saw her at the table.

"She cut herself," Lucas said. "She's okay. Just a little shook. We're going to do dinner, though. You and me. Okay?" Lucas put his hand on Gordon's shirt, pushed him up to the counter.

He stood at the counter, confused, half-grinning and

half-frowning, a big kid a thousand miles from home standing in a strange kitchen, looking at the bloody knife the woman that he loved had just used to cut herself, and at the food, red, white, green, gold, that she had cut with such care into wedges and slices and shapes revealing an unbearable sort of perfection, scattered over the kitchen counter. The kid was staring at them.

"Beautiful, aren't they?" Lucas said, and he saw the kid's eyes soften. "Let's get to work here." He picked up the knife and dropped it into the sink. "And I'll tell you stuff. Like, what happens to a genius." He turned the tap on.

Lucas saw twenty years into the future, saw the kid standing, with a puzzled look, just as he was now, but smoking, at some window somewhere, thinking about this particular lie, the one he was telling him.

"You know what happens to a genius?" Lucas put his hand on the faucet handle, looked at Gordon, smiled. "Nothing," he said, shaking his head. He turned the water off. He shook his head again. "Absolutely nothing. So, the *first thing* all us geniuses do… is relax."

Gordon was nodding. Without being told to, he had begun herding the cut vegetables into groups, delicately guiding them through the debris on the counter with a fork, whispering.